Triangle

JON RIPSLINGER

HARCOURT BRACE & COMPANY
San Diego   New York   London

Requests for permission to make copies of any part of the work
should be mailed to: Permissions Department,
Harcourt Brace & Company, 6277 Sea Harbor Drive,
Orlando, Florida 32887–6777.

Library of Congress Cataloging-in-Publication Data
Ripslinger, Jon.
Triangle/Jon Ripslinger.—1st ed.
p. cm.
Summary: Eighteen-year-old Jeremy begins a secret affair with
Joy, the girlfriend of his paralyzed best friend, which threatens
to endanger her chances of leading her softball team
to victory in the state tournament.
ISBN 0-15-200048-8—ISBN 0-15-200049-6 (pbk.)
[1. Physically handicapped—Fiction. 2. Friendship—Fiction.
3. Pregnancy—Fiction. 4. Softball—Fiction.] I. Title.
PZ8.R485Tr 1994
[Fic]—dc20   93-20983

Printed in Hong Kong

Designed by Lori J. McThomas

First edition
A B C D E

To my wife, Colette, with love

Special thanks to
B. J. Doyen
Erin DeWitt
Dennis Sievers
Aaron King
Jane Ripslinger-Kroening
and
Jill Ripslinger

Triangle

Prologue

Joy Kelley's telephone call the night of the accident rocked me. I was home sacked out on the couch with the TV on when the call came at 1:00 A.M. Joy was crying so hard into the phone and my brain was so sleepy I thought something had happened to her. A chill of fear shot up my spine.

"Are you all right?" I said. "What's wrong?"

"I'm all right. It's Darin, Jeremy . . . he—" She broke off, unable to go on.

"Joy, what is it? What's happened?"

"It's Darin," she sobbed. "He's in the hospital. . . . Oh, God . . ."

"Hospital?"

"I'm with his parents. I thought you'd want to know. . . . There's been an accident." She started sobbing louder.

"Look, Joy . . . be cool. Be calm. What kind of accident? A car accident? Was he drinking?"

"His pool . . . the pool in his backyard . . ."

That's all I could get out of her.

"Where are you?" I said.

"Mercy . . . Mercy Hospital."

"I'll be there."

I was sixteen then, going to be a junior—for the first time in my life armed with a driver's license, blessed with freedom. Mom and I lived above the Uptown Tavern, which she owned. I flew down the stairs to the smoky bar, where she was filling mugs of beer for customers. I told her what had happened and asked if I could go to Riverbend.

She said, "Darin's been in an accident? How awful."

"Can I go, Mom?" I rattled my keys in my hand.

"Of course. Don't drive too fast."

As I drove my old Buick into the warm July night, I wondered what could have happened to Darin. He was my best friend; Joy was his girlfriend. Had he slipped and fallen on the pool deck? Had he broken an arm? A leg?

By my standards, Joy was the most beautiful girl in the world and the soon-to-be best high school softball pitcher in the state; but she was emotional, excitable. Maybe she had freaked out over nothing. Maybe Darin had sprained his big toe.

When I arrived at the hospital, I found Darin's father, Mr. Steele, and Joy seated in a small waiting room near the intensive care unit on the fourth floor. I realized that whatever had happened to Darin was more serious than I'd thought. I swallowed and walked into the deadly silent room.

Mr. Steele sat on the edge of a chair, elbows on his knees, head hanging, clenching and unclenching his hands. The pale light from a table lamp cast his shadow on the carpeting.

I stood over him. "What is it, Mr. Steele? What happened?"

He looked at me, his beard a gray stubble, his dull gray eyes red-rimmed and glassy. He'd been crying, but he'd also been drinking. I smelled booze on him mingled with the scent of pipe tobacco. He always drank.

"What happened?" I said again.

Darin's dead—the most horrible answer of all flashed in my brain.

"An accident," Mr. Steele said in a flat voice.

"Where's Mrs. Steele?"

"With Darin. They'll let only one of us in with him at a time."

Joy began to sob quietly, and I turned to her. She sat on a couch across the room, a magazine-littered table in front of her knees. My heart wrenched. I hated seeing her in pain. She was Darin's girlfriend, but I loved her more than he did, had loved her secretly for a long while.

I shoved the table aside and dropped to one knee in front of her.

"Joy, what is it?" I took her sweaty hands into mine and held them tightly, trying to stop them from trembling.

"D-Darin's still unconscious." Her voice was a shaky whisper.

"What happened?" Tears crept into my eyes.

She began to hiccup, and I patted her softly on the back. "We were swimming in the pool," she said. "Just messing around. He . . . he dove into the shallow end."

I couldn't believe it. "Why?" I said. "What was he thinking?"

Joy squeezed my hands and tears dropped from her blue eyes.

"What were you guys doing?" I said. "Was he drinking?"

"Oh, Jeremy . . ."

"Tell me."

Before Joy could answer, Mrs. Steele appeared in the doorway. She looked pale, gaunt, haggard, but no tears flooded her dark eyes. While the rest of us were falling apart, she was in control of herself. She had to be strong for Darin's sake. I admired her.

She took a step into the room and shot Mr. Steele a long, ugly, disgusted gaze. "Look at you," she said. "Look at you. Drunk!"

"I'm sorry," he whispered.

"I can't count on you. I can *never* count on you."

Mr. Steele's head dropped miserably, and his eyes closed.

I felt sorry for him. I cleared my throat. "How's Darin?" I squeezed Joy's hand, and she held her breath.

"He's conscious," Mrs. Steele said through tight lips.

"Thank God," Mr. Steele mumbled. He started to shake.

"Great," I said quietly. "Hear that, Joy?"

"Yes," she whispered.

"He realizes he's in the hospital," Mrs. Steele said, "but he doesn't know why. He can't remember what happened." Mrs. Steele's eyes landed on Joy, and she hurled each word at Joy as if it were a stone. "They think his neck is broken. Paralyzed from the neck down."

Joy caught her breath and gasped, "Oh, no . . ."

I stiffened, resenting Mrs. Steele's harshness.

Covering her face with her hands, Joy began to sob again. I eased next to her on the couch, my arm circling her shoulders, pulling her close to me. I blinked and tears ran down my cheeks.

"They won't know for several days the extent of his injuries or anything about the paralysis." Mrs. Steele's lips quivered, for the first time showing her own emotion. "But . . . but he's alive," she murmured. "He's alive."

"Thank God," Mr. Steele mumbled again.

"Amen," I answered and held Joy tighter, trying to soothe her pain.

I'll stick by you, Joy. I love you.

Chapter 1

JOY KELLEY STOOD ON THE MOUND AND GLOWERED AT the burly Centerville cleanup hitter. The girl stepped into the batter's box, waving her bat, wiggling her butt. Dust exploded from Joy's glove each time she slammed the ball into the pocket.

"Throw the heater, Joy!" Darin hollered.

He sat next to me in his wheelchair. Bracketed to the back of his chair, a green-and-white striped umbrella shaded Darin from the July sun. Iowa was one of the few states that played summer softball so that during the spring girls could go out for track, golf, or tennis. Even graduated seniors like Joy were eligible for summer ball.

"Throw strikes!" I yelled from my lawn chair, where I kept a play-by-play book. I also charted Joy's pitches: how many, what kind, how many balls and strikes. We sat behind the fence, close to third base. "C'mon, Joy! C'mon, babe!"

I knew Joy could throw a softball sixty miles per hour. The problem was, when she was rattled she didn't throw strikes. She was rattled this Wednesday afternoon. Clinging to a 2–1 lead in the bottom of the seventh, she faced Centerville's cleanup hitter with the bases loaded and two outs. A trip to the finals of the Iowa girls' state softball tournament hung in the balance.

"God, Jeremy," Darin said, "she can't let this game slip away. What's wrong with her?"

"Two–one in the bottom of the seventh, two out, then an infield error and two walks—wouldn't you be a little shaken?" I said. "Besides, it's hot. She's already thrown ninety-six pitches. She's tired."

"You always make excuses for her."

"I understand her."

"Strike the moose out!" Darin screamed at Joy. Then to me, "Look at the batter's size. She should be swinging a telephone pole."

Joy took the sign from the catcher and nodded. Her windmill delivery zoomed the ball low and inside.

"Ball!" barked the umpire behind the plate.

The batter stepped out of the box and nodded approval. Shawna snapped the ball back to Joy. Tall, sinewy, with blond hair in a ponytail, Joy stalked around the mound, kicking at the rubber, mumbling to herself.

Darin shook his head. "She's going to lose it. We need one more out, but she's going to lose it. You can kiss a spot in the state tournament good-bye."

"Cool it, OK? She got us this far."

"Yeah, well, I've seen her blow a few games."

"She's tired, I'm telling you. It's ninety-five degrees, probably a hundred-ten on the mound."

"Give me a break!"

"She's releasing the ball too soon. That's why her fastball is dropping low and inside to a right-handed batter."

"Jeremy, I *hate* it when you sound as if you know everything. The truth is she hasn't got it in the clutch."

I licked my lips, tasting dust. "C'mon, Joy!"

Joy gripped the ball in her glove and stared at the hitter, Joy's grimy face like stone. The front of her green-and-white uniform—chest, belly, thighs—was covered with dirt because she had dived into home to score the go-ahead run in the top of the sixth. She stepped onto the rubber, leaned forward, strode, and fired a fastball at the knees. "Ball two!" cried the ump.

"What?!" screamed Darin. "That pig's blind!"

Maple Grove fans in the bleachers behind third base jumped up, cupped their hands around their mouths, and booed. In the brutal heat most of the kids wore shorts—girls in sleeveless T-shirts, tank tops, and halters; boys bare-chested, T-shirts dangling from back pockets. Parents shaded their eyes from the sun with sunglasses, straw hats, and baseball caps.

Coach Thorton called time out and walked slowly to the mound to talk to Joy and give her a chance to collect herself. Shawna trotted to the mound from her catcher's spot, and Corky Robinson came in from third base to join the conference.

"They can't put Meyer in," Darin said. "She's got a sore shoulder. Besides, she's a sophomore; she'd wet her pants."

"If he's smart, he'll tell Joy to sneak a breaking ball in, then come back with the drop, get the batter to ground out."

"You know it all, don't you?"

I know Joy better than you ever will.

"I know the game better than Thorton does," I said.

And I knew what Thorton was probably telling Joy. Instead of telling her to relax, take it easy, he was putting more pressure on her, reminding her this was the first time the Maple Grove softball team had had a chance at the state finals. He was telling her, "Bear down, get tough. Use that fastball. Blow this ox away."

"Play ball," the ump called and dusted off the plate with his whisk broom.

As the conference broke up, Thorton sauntered back to the dugout, clapping.

Joy wiped the sweat off her forehead with the back of her hand. Above her, the fierce blue sky pulsed with heat, and she looked pale, as if she were going to faint.

Joy slammed the ball into her glove. The batter dug in at the plate, wiggling her butt again. She looked like a fullback.

"C'mon, babe!" Jeremy yelled.

Joy fired. Her fastball bounced in front of the plate, skipping to Shawna's right. Only Shawna's desperate lunge for the ball—she got her glove on it—stopped it from rolling to the backstop. The third-base runner broke for home, but when she saw Joy racing to cover the plate, she dove back to third.

"Ball three!" Darin screamed, echoing the ump's call. "I need a beer."

I swallowed, my throat itchy and dry. Coach Thorton motioned the infield a little farther back, making it easier to field a hot ground ball for a force out at any base. The outfield played straight away and deep, hoping to snare a smash off the hitter's bat. A walk or a bloop single spelled disaster.

"Swing, batter-batter-batter," our infield cat-called.

I watched Centerville's coach at third flash signals to his hitter. She waved the bat menacingly. She'd touched Joy for a double in the fifth inning, driving in Centerville's only run. I'm sure the coach was telling her to take the next pitch. Why swing and pop up or ground out? A walk was as good as a hit.

"Lay one in there, Joy," I yelled. "She's not going to swing."

"Throw the heater, Joy!" Darin screamed. "Strike her out!"

Joy delivered a half-speed fastball, down the pipe, belt high. The batter tensed, strode forward—I could almost see her lick her lips, she wanted a piece of that pitch so badly—but she let it go by.

"Strike!" said the ump.

The Centerville coach signaled again. Joy would have to make a better pitch this time. The hitter might go for a fat 3–1 pitch like the last one and blast it out of here. The Maple Grove season would be over.

"Curve ball!" I yelled.

"Swing, batter-batter-batter!" our infield chanted.

"Throw heat!" Darin screamed.

The way Joy gripped the ball, grimacing, gritting her teeth, I knew she was going to challenge the hitter with another fastball—Thorton's decision. It was the wrong pitch. I felt my heart in my throat.

"Swing, batter-batter-batter!"

Joy's fastball came in letter high across the plate. The Centerville hitter smashed a screaming line drive. From her vicious swing and the *clunk* of the ball off the aluminum bat, I could tell the ball was destined for the left-field corner, a base-clearing double or triple, but the smash was right at third baseman Corky Robinson. Throwing her gloved hand high, she speared the drive, nearly tumbled over backward, but held on.

I slumped in my chair. The game was over. Maple Grove had won 2–1.

Fans from both teams sat stunned into a moment's silence, neither group believing what had happened. Then suddenly our fans were jumping up and down in the bleachers, pounding the air with fists clenched above their heads, shouting: "We're number one! We're number one!" The players in our dugout rushed screaming onto the field and, along with the starters, swarmed Corky—fifteen girls, leaping into the air, hugging each other, tumbling and falling onto the ground, laughing, crying, shrieking.

"I can't believe it," Darin said, his head jerking. It often jerked when he was nervous, excited, or drunk.

"We did it." I let out a long, low breath.

"She'll have to pitch better next week," Darin said.

"Something's wrong with her."

"It's the pressure. She can't take the pressure."

What do you know about her?

"Maybe she's tired," I said. "That's all. Tired."

Chapter 2

AFTER OUR FANS CLEARED OFF THE FIELD AND THE dust settled, the players from each team lined up to shake hands with each other, and then officials made the presentation of trophies for first, second, and third places in the regional tournament. All smiles, Joy, Shawna, and Corky held the first-place trophy on home plate, Coach Thorton standing behind them, while photographers snapped pictures.

While that was going on, I figured the game totals. I knew Joy's dad would be looking over my shoulder any minute, wanting to check his totals with mine. A short but wiry, smiling, red-faced Irishman, he was sports editor for the *Riverbend Times*. Fifteen miles north of Maple Grove, Riverbend was the site of next week's state finals.

I felt a hand on my shoulder and knew Mr. Kelley stood beside me.

Darin said to him, "Joy nearly blew it."

"It's a team game, coach. Remember that." Mr. Kelley called everyone "coach" except Joy and his wife.

Looking over my shoulder, he said, "So what have you got for totals?"

"We got two runs on six hits, two walks, and an error," I said.

"Joy pitched a three-hitter?" he asked.

"Three hits."

"Eight walks?"

"Ten," I said.

"You sure?"

"Positive. Two in the first, one in the third—"

"OK. How many strikeouts?"

"Those walks kept her in trouble," Darin said. "She's getting worse."

"She'll be all right," Mr. Kelley said. "How many strikeouts?"

"Ten," I said.

"That's what I've got, coach." He smiled at me. "You should become a sports reporter, not a sailor."

Suddenly Joy was at our side, beaming but exhausted, her face pale and dirty, sweat beading her forehead. A summer of playing softball in the sun had turned her hair corn-silk blond, leaving faint

shades of red. Loose wet strands curled on her forehead and around her ears. Mrs. Kelley stood beside
Joy, holding Joy's glove.

When Mr. Kelley stood up, Joy draped her arms
around his neck. She was a head taller than her dad.
"Oh, Daddy, we made it! We're in the state finals!"

"You bet, killer. And when we win it all and I
finish writing about you, every college in the country
will be offering you a scholarship."

"Especially Iowa!" Darin said.

"Especially Iowa!" Mr. Kelley agreed.

Lots of college scouts had shown an interest in
Joy last year, her junior year; but when Riverbend
West blasted her off the mound and she lost the first
game of the district tournament, interest trailed off.
If she could win the state tournament this year, she'd
be back in the hunt for a ride to a major school.
Scouts from Iowa, Nebraska, and Oklahoma always
kept a close eye on the Iowa tournament and handed
out a scholarship or two.

"How about a kiss?" As Darin lifted his arms to
reach Joy, his mouth twisted eagerly.

Joy hadn't looked at me. She bent under the umbrella to give Darin a kiss on the cheek, but he circled
her neck with his arms and pulled her head down
for a real kiss.

I turned away.

Mrs. Kelley was watching me. A tall blond like

Joy, but plump with red cheeks, she had been my sophomore math teacher. "How do the stats look?" she said.

"Not bad. Ten strikeouts"—I shrugged—"ten walks."

"I'd settle for half the strikeouts and half the walks."

"You've got that right," I said. Mrs. Kelley always made sense.

"It was so hot out there!" Joy finally smiled at me. Her eyes were a deep blue flecked with gold, her eyelashes so light they seemed bleached.

I stood up and smiled back. "Congratulations." I thrust out my hand.

Joy gripped it. Though her hand was slender with long fingers and short nails, her grip was a vise. This was a hand that could throw fastballs, curves, drops, change-ups; it was a hand that would probably bring Joy Kelley college fame; maybe even earn her a chance to coach at a college or university.

I squeezed her hand softly, and we shook. "You did a nice job. You kept your cool."

"I was so afraid I was going to blow it."

"You don't concentrate," Darin said. "You let everything bother you."

Lay off her!

"I think it's been a long, difficult tournament," Mrs. Kelley said. "Now we've got a six-hour drive home. You young people should be home early tonight. What do you say?" Mrs. Kelley glanced at me: I was always the designated driver.

"I agree," I said.

"No parties," she said.

"Mom!" Joy groaned. "We're not high school kids anymore. We've graduated."

"You're playing for a high school team. You're not twenty-one. Only eighteen."

"I'm nineteen," Darin piped up.

"That's not twenty-one," Mrs. Kelley reminded him. "You can celebrate after we win the state tournament. That's time enough."

"Let's get." Mr. Kelley snapped his game book closed. "I've got a story to file."

"Hey, Joy! The bus is ready to leave!" Corky yelled.

Looking apologetic, Joy stroked Darin's cheek. "I've got to go back on the bus."

"It's a stupid rule." Darin's head jerked. "You ought to tell Thorton to kiss off."

"He wants us all on the bus," Joy said. "There's nothing I can do."

"Let's get going." I folded my lawn chair, then released the umbrella from Darin's chair and snapped it down.

"Meet me at school in the parking lot?" Joy said.

"We'll be there." I released the brake on Darin's chair.

"Don't take all night showering and dressing."

Darin tried to grab Joy's wrist so he could pull her close for a second kiss, but she pulled her hand away and tousled his shoulder-length black hair. Before his accident, two years ago, when he was a jock, Darin wore a crew cut, and he wouldn't have been caught dead wearing a diamond earring in his left ear, as he did now.

"I won't be long." Joy kissed him lightly on the forehead. "See you guys." She smiled again, her eyes the brightest, clearest eyes I'd ever seen, her mouth perfect.

"See you," I said.

I knew I'd always love her.

Chapter 3

"I NEED A BEER," DARIN SAID.

"Got some iced in the van," I told him.

Lugging my chair, game book, pitching charts, and Darin's umbrella, I pushed him in his wheelchair across the blacktop parking lot behind Centerville High School.

Maple Leaf fans walked briskly by, laughing and high-fiving each other, while Centerville fans grumbled about luck and scowled at anyone wearing green-and-white Maple Leaf colors—which included Darin and me: green shorts, white T-shirts.

Darin's pointed elbows and knees looked like sticks ready to poke through his pale skin. Before the accident, Darin had been a three-sport athlete: football, wrestling, track. He had been muscular, broad-shouldered, and narrow-waisted. A fierce and aggressive athlete, he weighed 180 then; now he was 95, thin and fragile, though he was improving rapidly, gaining weight and strength, due to a recent operation and intensive therapy.

In fact, eighteen months ago he had come home from the hospital a quadriplegic in a breath-operated wheelchair. Now he used a regular chair and wheeled himself around his house with great mobility, but pushing him at games was easier and faster for both of us.

Specially equipped, Darin's blue Ford conversion van was state of the art. Unlocking the side door, I slid it open, and grabbed the control cord, lowering the hydraulic lift to the ground. I clamped Darin's chair to the platform, then pushed the "raise" button on the cord. Humming, the lift hoisted him into the van. As soon as I got him settled with a cold beer in his hand, he frowned. "Coors? Where's the Bud?"

"I was in a hurry." I slid into the driver's captain's chair. "I grabbed the first thing I could find." I'd taken the twelve-pack from the cooler at my mom's tavern. That's where I got all the beer for Darin and Joy. I hardly ever drank it.

"Put the air on."

"Wait till I get the damn van started."

Lately, Darin had been trying my patience. I don't know how I'd stayed friends with him this long after the accident. I don't think he realized how critical and abusive he had become to the people who loved him. It was as if the chair were slowly changing him, and he was powerless to do anything about it. There was a time when Darin laughed, joked, and teased; he could be warm and sympathetic. But not recently. The worst part for me was the way he treated Joy—as if he owned her, as if she were his slave, always incredibly hard on her.

"So what do you think is wrong with her?" Darin asked.

I was trying to nose the van into the single lane of traffic headed out of the parking lot. Recognizing the van as Darin's, a Maple Leaf fan driving a red Camaro let us in, horn hooting.

I waved thanks. "It's the heat," I said, and leaned on the van's horn, joining the chorus.

"I've seen her pitch on hotter days than this."

"That was during the middle of the season," I said. "This is the end of the season. Have you ever thought that she's worn-out? Her season began in December with weight lifting. She started throwing in February, working up to throwing an hour a day, five days a week."

"Don't give me that. What it boils down to is she needs to shape up and win the state tournament or she probably won't get a scholarship to Iowa. Her won-lost record isn't that great."

"Just because you're going to Iowa—"

"I want her with me. What's she supposed to do, join the navy with you?"

"There are other schools besides Iowa."

"But they're not where *I'm* going!"

"Let me tell you something about her record. She's pitched two perfect games this season. In one she struck out twenty-one batters."

"Against a little Catholic school."

"So what? She has four one-hitters and ten shut-outs. In thirty-nine games—including today's— she's struck out over four hundred. That's an average of almost two per inning."

"I hate it when you try to impress me with stats. That's all you've got on the brain—stats."

"I'm not trying to impress you. I'm giving you the facts."

"Yeah, well, the fact is Joy's record is 30–8. That's not so hot. Hightower is 35–4, and she's beat Joy twice this season."

"Joy is 31–8. She won today, remember?"

"Drop dead!"

"She's won her last seven games," I reminded him.

"How many walks does she give up a game? How many games has she lost because she walked the winning run in? You treat her like a baby. She needs somebody on her case all the time."

She needs love.

"Hey, man, she's human," I said. "Everybody puts so much pressure on her. And you're the worst."

"Drop dead!" he said again. "Get me another beer."

Darin and I didn't talk after that. I pulled over to the side of the road, crawled in back and got another beer for him from the cooler. I turned on the ten-inch color TV built into the van's ceiling and tuned in the Cub–Cardinal doubleheader. The Cards had won the first game; the second one was just starting. Darin hated the Cubs and loved the Redbirds. I knew the game, a beer, and the possibility of a Card sweep would keep him occupied.

While I drove through Centerville, a thought flashed through my mind, a thought that had been recurring more often lately, one that never failed to frighten me, sending shivers up my spine: *Someday I'm going to tell you about Joy and me, Darin. I really am.*

Chapter 4

TEN MINUTES AFTER TURNING THE CARD–CUB GAME on for Darin, I caught up with the convoy of Maple Grove cars speeding home on Highway 34, a hilly two-lane blacktop snaking east. On either side of the highway, fields of corn stretched as far as the eye could see. Ahead of me, twenty-five or thirty cars gleamed in the sun, green-and-white streamers flying from windows and whipping in the wind.

The rides home next week after the tournament games would be shorter: Riverbend was only a ten- to twelve-minute drive from Maple Grove, depending on how fast you liked to go. Better yet, since three Riverbend schools belonged to the Mississippi Valley Conference along with Maple Grove, our girls had played at their stadium many times. The Leafs would feel as if they had a home-field advantage over other teams. Except for the Riverbend West Falcons.

In the rearview mirror I glanced at Darin—beer clutched in his hand, eyes glued to the TV.

"Comfortable?" I asked.

"I'll live."

Riverbend is where Darin, Joy, and I met for the first time—at the municipal swimming pool. That's where Maple Grove kids went to swim during the summer because Maple Grove was too small to have its own pool. Once a week on Wednesdays, we piled onto a school bus that hauled us to the Riverbend pool.

Darin's folks had just moved to Maple Grove; their new house with its swimming pool wasn't completed. Joy and I were nine years old, Darin, ten. Joy was going to St. Mary's, the Catholic elementary school, while I attended Maple Grove Elementary. We were all strangers.

We didn't meet till the three of us encountered Chase Saunders in the pool. A ninth-grade Maple Grove bully, fat and stupid, Chase was ducking kids underwater and pulling everyone's swimsuit down. When he did it to me, I crawled out of the pool and complained tearfully to the lifeguard: "That kid's not nice."

She gave me a tired look. "Get lost, kid."

Darin also stood in front of her stand, his feet

planted firmly on the concrete deck, hands locked on his hips, demanding something be done. "That guy's pulling our pants down!" he yelled.

The lifeguard studied her painted nails a moment, then brushed her hair away from her face. "Why don't you wusses play in the kiddie pool?" she said. "Leave the big kids alone."

Darin's deep-set dark eyes flashed angrily. "Tell the big kids to leave *us* alone!" he shouted at her.

"The kiddie pool or get out!" She eyed a high school stud strolling up to her stand. He glanced at Darin and me, his scowl telling us to get lost. Then he traced his index finger down the lifeguard's leg.

"You're hot, Gloria."

"You don't have to tell me that."

Grumbling, Darin and I went back to the adult pool and stood at the edge—I was starting to shiver—looking for Saunders. I prayed he'd gone away. He hadn't. He surfaced in front of us, in about four feet of water, laughing, wiping his face. An instant later, Joy exploded out of the water and smashed him in the face with a vicious right. "Leave me alone!" she yelled at Chase.

He'd messed with the wrong person.

"Let's get 'im!" Darin said.

He leapt from the edge of the pool onto Saunders's back, one arm wrapped around Saunders's neck, his legs wrapped around the bully's fat belly. While I watched from the deck, amazed, frightened, and shivering, Darin beat on Saunders's head with his free hand as Joy smacked him in the face again. Suddenly I took courage and did the bravest thing I'd ever done in my life to that point: I dove into the water, grabbed Saunders's ankle with both hands, and bit him on the calf.

Later, the head lifeguard kicked Joy, Darin, and me out of the pool. "I don't want to see you creeps again today!"

"Don't worry!" Darin snorted. "You'll never see me again. I'm going to have my own pool!"

After showering, dressing, and leaving the pool, we had to sit on the bus till four o'clock, when the rest of the kids would be ready to go home. While the bus driver slept, we played on the bus, mixing up pairs of kids' sandals and flip-flops that they'd left behind, yelling "Jerk!" out the window at people who walked by, then ducking down in the seat.

Soon Joy and Darin sat alone in the back of the bus, talking and laughing. I had ceased to exist. At that time in my life, I didn't have any friends. I was a basic nerd: skinny with glasses, round shouldered, butched hair. I didn't want to blow the possibility of gaining two friends, so after the bus dropped us off at the town square in Maple Grove, I coaxed Joy and Darin to cross the street to my mom's tavern.

We stood underneath the Budweiser sign that hung from the front of the building over the sidewalk. "She won't care if you come in. I bring friends here all the time," I lied. The hot sidewalk cement burned my feet through my thin-soled Nikes.

"You're sure it's your mom's tavern?" Joy said. "You're not lying?"

"Positive. We live upstairs. Ask her."

"Will your mom give us free pop and stuff?" Darin said.

"Maybe."

Darin nudged Joy with his elbow. "Let's go in."

Mom treated us with candy and pop and potato chips. Tired of seeing my face stuck in a book, she was happy to entertain my two new friends.

"My house is going to have a pool." Darin munched a Snickers as we sat at a table, candy and pop in front of us. "You guys can come over whenever you want to. I mean it."

"That'll be great." I chewed a stick of black licorice. "I've never swum in anybody's pool. Only the Riverbend pool."

"It'll beat the Riverbend pool," Darin said.

"I'll be there every day," Joy said, and swigged Pepsi.

I brought Darin and Joy to the tavern a lot that summer, especially in the afternoons when only a few old-timers played cards in a smoky corner. Later in the summer, when his folks' new house was finished, we swam nearly every day in Darin's pool.

"How about another cold beer!" Darin demanded.

"Why don't you wait?" Pulling up behind me, three more Maple Grove cars had joined our triumphant going-home convoy. Brilliant red in a blue sky, the sun was settling in the west, casting long car shadows on the shoulder of the road.

"Wait for what?" Darin said. "Beer was meant to be drunk."

"Not all at once."

"Just *do* it, will you?" he exploded. "I hate people controlling my life, telling me what I can and can't do. Get me a beer."

Flashing my right-turn signal, I pulled off the road. Gravel pinged off the van's aluminum running boards as I braked on the shoulder. The three cars behind me zoomed by. I decided to drag the cooler up from the rear of the van and set it next to Darin so he could drink all the beer he wanted.

Chapter 5

In Maple Grove, I guided Darin's van into the McDonald's drive-thru lane at 9:00 p.m. Kids called the place the Mac Shack; it was the only fast-food place in town. The night was almost fully dark, the Shack's red-and-yellow neon lights glaring through the windshield. I was starved. Darin had downed at least six beers before falling asleep. I hoped he'd stay asleep till after I picked up Joy at school and took him home. Then I could be alone with her, but as I pulled up to the drive-thru speaker to order, I heard him mumbling, "Where are we?"

"Cardinals won the second game 6–4," I said, and looked in the rearview mirror as he swiped the back of his hand across his mouth.

"I figured they would." He yawned, blinked, scowled. "Where are we?" he said again.

"The Shack. What do you want to eat?"

"Nothing."

"You're getting something anyway."

I ordered three Big Macs, three fries, and three chocolate milkshakes. I figured Joy would be hungry, too. I paid, then drove seven blocks to the Maple Grove High School parking lot. Even though the team bus hadn't made it yet, the lot had filled with carloads of fans—car lights on, horns blaring—waiting to congratulate the team. The evening remained hot and humid, so for Darin's comfort I kept the van doors closed, the motor running, and the air-conditioning humming. When I flicked on the dome light, Darin squinted at the yellow glow as if it were a spotlight.

"I think I'll have a beer," he said and blinked, his eyes red-rimmed and glassy.

I got up and moved the cooler out of his reach. "You're drunk. You better eat something." I sat down again.

His head jerked. "What did I tell you? I can't stand people telling me what I can and can't do."

I opened the warm McDonald's bag and the mixed aroma of Big Macs and fries escaped into the van. "If there's a beer left, you can have it after you eat."

"Who gives you the right to tell me—?"

"Eat!"

I knew I was making him mad, but I didn't care. I handed Darin's Big Mac to him, paper carefully wrapped around the bottom half so catsup and mustard wouldn't drip. "How about some french fries?" I said.

He glared at me. He knew I wasn't kidding about his eating before I let him have a beer. "A few," he said.

A year ago, when he couldn't use his arms, I often fed Darin like a baby, holding a burger to his mouth so he could take a bite, then wiping his lips with a napkin. Now he managed by himself.

He sipped his shake through a straw and made a face. "A beer would taste better."

"You've got only one liver. You want to paralyze that, too?"

"Drop dead!"

I spotted the team bus wheeling into the parking lot, lights flashing across the parked cars. Before it even stopped, screaming fans poured out of their cars, then mobbed the girls as they jumped off the bus. Fans set off firecrackers. As soon as Joy could break away from the crowd, she'd head for the showers and then be back out.

Sure enough, fifteen minutes later, Joy came rushing through the school doors toward the van, dressed in shorts and a T-shirt, her gym bag slung over her shoulder, banging off her hip as she ran. She whipped open the van's sliding door, letting in a puff of warm air, and jumped in, tossing her gym bag into the back.

"Wow! Is it cool in here!" She sat on the edge of the passenger's captain's chair. Still wet, her blond hair was pulled straight back and tied at the base of her neck with a white ribbon. "And it smells good, too. Hamburgers? French fries?"

"A Big Mac, fries, and a milkshake," I said. "Got yours right here in the bag."

"A kiss?" Darin said. "Do I rate a kiss? Who do you think rooted hard enough for you to win?"

"Both of you," Joy said, laughing, half standing, stretching to kiss Darin. "And a kiss for Jeremy, too." She kissed me lightly on the cheek. I inhaled her scent, shuddering. After showering, she must have dabbed perfume behind her ears, on her throat.

"How you feeling?" I asked her.

"All right."

"Your arm?"

"Fine. They packed it in ice on the way home."

"You looked terrible out there," Darin said.

"Give her a break!" I shot him a look. "It was hot."

"So? She still looked terrible."

"I felt drained," Joy said, then added sheepishly, "I forgot my Dramamine. I got sick on the bus."

I rolled my eyes. "Was that your problem?"

"I think so."

"Man, how could you do that?"

Joy's face flushed. "I was in a hurry and forgot, that's all. Mom takes the same pills. She gave me some after the game. I was OK on the way home."

"I never thought about your getting bus sick."

Joy leaned back in her seat and stretched her bare legs. "That error and those two walks really hurt," she said. "I got rattled. God, I always get rattled. I thought I was going to lose it for sure. My knees were actually shaking."

"The error wasn't your fault," I said, "and the defense came through. You won, that's all that counts."

"You'll have to do better next week," Darin said.

"She will." I handed Joy the McDonald's bag with her food in it. Then I flipped off the dome light, released the van's emergency brake, and shifted into gear. "Let's get out of here."

"You want a beer?" Darin asked Joy.

"A milkshake's fine," Joy said between bites of her Big Mac.

While kids piled into cars and revved motors, I pulled out of the parking lot and headed for Darin's house. Rosy streetlights glowed softly through the trees.

"Let's hit some parties," Darin said. "We're regional champs; there's got to be parties everywhere, even if it is Wednesday night."

"I'm really tired," Joy said. "And we've got practice at eight in the morning."

"So?" Darin said. "That hasn't bothered you
before."

Joy sipped her milkshake through a straw. "These
are big games coming up, the biggest in my life. I
think my mother's right. No parties. I should get
home early."

"I'm taking both of you home," I told Darin over
my shoulder.

A moment's silence hung in the van; then Darin
suddenly screamed at the back of my head: "I *hate*
both of you jerks!"

"Darin!"

"Ignore him," I said. "He's still drunk."

Setting her shake and Big Mac on the floor, Joy
got up and moved to where Darin sat. "Be quiet,"
she said softly.

"I hate you! Do you hear! *Both* of you! God, I
can't take this: trapped in this chair, not being able
to do what *I* want to do!"

I tried to keep one eye on the street ahead and
the other on the rearview mirror so I could see what
was happening in back. His head twitching and jerking, Darin pounded the arms of his chair with his
fists. "You're *jerks!*"

Kneeling on one knee, Joy cupped Darin's face in
her hands. "Listen to me, honey. I've got practice

tomorrow, I'm tired. You've already had enough to drink."

"You have no right to tell me—"

She smothered his words with a kiss. I glanced at the road, then into the rearview mirror again. She was kissing his lips, his forehead, his cheeks. Instead of screaming, Darin was suddenly groaning and breathing heavily. I stared ahead at the street, trying to ignore their noises and concentrate on driving. Headlights burned my eyes and jealousy stabbed my heart. Both Darin and I were groaning. But for different reasons.

Chapter

6

DARIN'S FOLKS LIVED IN A BRICK HOME IN A SUB-
division called Sunnyside on the outskirts of Maple
Grove. Shrubs and flowers in tidy rows fronted the
house, and a wide expanse of green grass led to a
huge rectangular pool in the backyard. Adding pri-
vacy, a tall redwood fence surrounded the backyard.
Darin's father was a dentist; his mother had been a
personnel director at a John Deere tractor plant, Maple Grove's chief employer. But she quit her job to
be home with Darin and take him to therapy each
day at Mercy Hospital in Riverbend.

Joy could never bring Darin home without stopping to visit with them; after all, perhaps someday
she'd be their daughter-in-law.

I lowered Darin out of the van with the lift. While

I cleaned the trash out of the van, Joy wheeled him up the ramp into the house. In the warm night air, the moon rode high and silvery, surrounded by stars. When I finished stuffing the trash into a plastic bag, I unlocked the trunk on my car—my old four-door silver Buick Century—and dropped the bag in, slamming the trunk. My car wasn't much, but it was mine; it was paid for, and it was reliable.

I didn't go through the Steeles' house but walked around it to the backyard pool and patio because I knew that's where everyone would be. Dark-haired and dark-eyed like Darin, perhaps forty-five, Mrs. Steele was a pool freak.

Nervous around Mrs. Steele, I stayed away from her as much as possible. I wasn't sure—maybe it was my imagination—but I thought she was hitting on me. Several times during the last months, after I'd dropped Darin off, she'd walked me to the front door, her hand on my shoulder or arm, and said she knew I was lonely; she was lonely, too; I should stop by more often—when Darin and Joy were out. If there was any problem on my mind, she was always there for me. Maybe she was just being friendly and my imagination was overly sexed.

I unlatched the wooden gate to the backyard and let it swing closed behind me. Yard lights lit the patio. Soft blue, red, and yellow lights circling the pool's perimeter reflected off the water. As soon as she saw me, Mrs. Steele called from the patio table where she was sitting with her husband, "Jeremy, we saw the score on television. Isn't it marvelous! Maple Grove—regional champions!"

"First time ever," I said, "and it was a thriller. But the results were never in doubt, were they?" I looked at Joy and smiled for her benefit.

She sat at the table with Mr. and Mrs. Steele, Darin next to her holding her hand. "The ending was a little scary," she admitted.

"That's no lie," Darin said.

"You three kids!" Mrs. Steele exclaimed, clapping. "There's nothing any one of you can't do when you set your mind to it. I'm so proud of you, Joy. So proud of *all* of you."

"Thank you," Joy said, and flushed a little.

"Was the game as close as the score?" Mr. Steele asked.

He snapped off the portable TV on the table. Built solid like Darin once was, nearly bald, Mr. Steele was a quiet, sometimes distant man with gray eyes who often sat and listened while others talked. Until a month ago, maybe longer, I seldom saw him without a tall glass of Scotch and water in one hand, his smelly pipe in the other. Early in the morning, late at night, he was always sipping at a drink, though I'd never seen him abusive, maybe a little sarcastic sometimes, his words thick. Now he drank sparkling mineral water. He was always uncapping one of the eight-ounce bottles and pouring the water over ice, as if it were Scotch. And he didn't smoke anymore.

"I nearly blew the game," Joy said.

"You're not kidding," Darin added.

"We had a 2–1 lead going into the bottom of the seventh," I began explaining. Then Darin and Joy jumped in with their versions of the error, two walks, and final out. While they were yakking, contradicting one another, my eyes ventured toward Mrs. Steele's long, tanned legs, toenails painted brilliant red. She spotted my gaze and smiled. I jerked my eyes away. Part of my problem with Mrs. Steele was that although I stayed away from her, I could never take my eyes off her.

Mrs. Steele said, "Well, we won. That's all that matters." She patted Joy's hand. "I know you'll get a scholarship to Iowa and be with Darin. Won't that be wonderful?"

Mr. Steele sipped his mineral water. "Provided she wants to go there."

"She'll get scholarship offers from Florida and California," I said, "where she can play year-round. Maybe she can try out for the Pan Am Games."

Mrs. Steele's penciled eyebrows arched. "I'm sure you want to go to Iowa, don't you, dear?" she asked Joy.

"Iowa would be great," Joy said.

"It's the only place for you," Darin said.

Mrs. Steele brushed her short black hair back with her hands, gold hoop earrings dangling, rings of diamond and turquoise on nearly every finger. "Darin would miss you, dear."

"Maybe Darin should be on his own," Mr. Steele said.

Darin scowled. "What do you know about it?" he said to his father.

Mrs. Steele ignored both remarks. "I was thinking the other day how lucky Darin is to have you two friends. I mean, after being out of school all that time, he worked hard and was able to graduate with his best friends. Both of you have been such a help."

Darin's head twitched. "These guys are jerks!"

"Sweetheart, that's not true!" Mrs. Steele gave him a stern look, then smiled at Joy and me. "He's joking. I think it's marvelous you three have been such close friends all these years, and there's never been a fight among you. And you're still such dear friends."

I let out a heavy sigh. "Look, it's late, nearly eleven. I should get going." I looked at Joy. "I'll give you a ride home."

"Stay," Darin said to her. "My mom can give you a ride."

"Certainly," Mrs. Steele said.

"It is late," Mr. Steele said. "Darin should go to bed."

"I'm not a kid!" Darin shouted. "I'll go to bed

when I want! Not when someone decides to *put* me there."

"You have therapy in the morning," Mr. Steele reminded him.

"Who cares?"

"Darin, stop!" Mrs. Steele rose from her chair.

Joy stroked his cheek. "Look, Darin, honey, it really is late. I'm beat." She bent and kissed him on the forehead.

"I'll wait for you in the car," I told Joy. "Good night, Mr. and Mrs. Steele." I patted Darin's shoulder. "See you, Darin."

Darin's face twisted abruptly. "Do you like taking my girl home at night?" he asked. "Do you have fun with her?"

My eyes darted toward Joy. Her expression remained carefully blank. "You're crazy," I said to Darin, but I couldn't look him in the eye.

"Right," he sneered. "Then why can't my mom take her home?"

"Darin! Apologize this minute," Mrs. Steele said.

"I don't care if your mother takes her home," I said. "I don't care if she walks. I don't care if she stays all night!"

"Like hell you don't!"

Face burning, I whirled and headed for the house. I was so mad I didn't think about walking around the outside of the house, the way I'd come. I was striding through the dark rec room when Mr. Steele called my name, "Jeremy, just a minute. Jeremy . . ." He was following behind me.

I stopped and turned. He flipped a switch that turned on a fluorescent light above the pool table and the beer signs behind the bar. He pointed at a chair. "Jeremy, sit down."

"No thanks, I'm leaving."

"Jeremy, I want to talk to you a moment."

"About what?" I swallowed. Maybe he knew about Joy and me.

"About Darin," he said.

"All right."

My eyes landed on a picture of Darin on the fireplace mantel. Taken when he was a junior, before the accident, it showed him in his football uniform, kneeling in green grass, holding his helmet in his right arm. His face was squared off with a wide mouth and pouty underlip. His deep-set dark eyes laughed, mocked. His muscular body, his strong chin—everything about Darin breathed confidence, determination, toughness. That was Darin then. He was different now.

"What about Darin?" I said.

"First, I . . . want to apologize for his remarks."

"You don't have to. Lately I don't take everything he says seriously."

"Good for you. I . . . don't know how to say this."

Mr. Steele seemed to falter. "Why don't you sit down?"

I hesitated a moment.

"Please?"

"All right." I eased onto the edge of a black leather lounge chair. "What is it?"

Mr. Steele took another sip of his mineral water and sat in a rocker by the stereo. "Darin's always been difficult, even before the accident, but lately he's been extremely difficult, abusive to both his mother and me."

"He gets into those moods once in a while," I said. "He'll be OK."

"I need your input, Jeremy. Do you have any idea why lately he's so moody, so irritable and critical?" Mr. Steele rocked back and forth slowly.

I shrugged. "I don't know. He shouldn't be, should he? I mean this last operation relieved a lot of pressure on his spinal cord, didn't it? He can use his arms and hands. He's gaining strength. He's improving every day, right?"

"Doctors say he's improving nicely. They think he'll walk someday."

"Then I don't know why he isn't more"—I wanted the right words—"more upbeat. I know he hates being told what to do."

"You remember when he first came home from the accident, a quadriplegic? How depressed he was?

He wanted to commit suicide, but he couldn't. He begged us all to kill him. You remember that?"

I studied the pattern in the light brown carpeting at my feet. "I remember," I said. "In fact one night he told me that you and Mrs. Steele were filthy rich, and he promised me his inheritance if I killed him. It was stupid, but I guess he was really desperate."

Mr. Steele stopped rocking and swirled the ice around in his glass. "Sometimes he brags about how tough he is. He talks about going to Iowa and earning a 4.0. He wants to be a lawyer. At other times he doesn't care. He dwells on lost opportunities rather than on the good fortune the future might bring. Lately, he isn't sleeping at night; he insists the TV in his room be left on. He won't eat. It's almost as if he's . . . manic-depressive." Mr. Steele watched for my reaction. "You know what that is?"

I shrugged again. "Sure. I read about it in psychology class. One day a person can be really high with feelings of elation and power, then the next day filled with feelings of depression and paranoia."

"That's right."

"And you think Darin's acting like that?"

Mr. Steele turned the glass in his hand. "I think it's the fact that everyone's going off to school in the fall looking forward to fulfilling high school dreams. Darin will be going off to school, too, but he'll be in a wheelchair. He won't come close to being what he wanted to be in college: a football star. He's just starting to fully realize that. It's getting to him."

"There's more to life than sports."

"There wasn't for Darin. Sports was all he ever talked about. All he ever did. You know that. He's lost everything. Except Joy, of course. He still has her. And you."

My feet shuffled nervously. "Yeah. He still has us."

"I think Joy's a big part of what's holding him together, but she has a right to her own life. She shouldn't be forced into going to Iowa if she doesn't want to."

"She won't. She has a mind of her own."

Mr. Steele drained his glass and stared at the ice in the bottom a moment. "Listen, Jeremy, I want to tell you something. A secret, sort of. And I want to ask a couple of favors."

I felt wary. "All right."

Mr. Steele stood up. "I've put all the pills in the house out of Darin's reach, butcher knives— everything."

I blinked. "Wait a minute. You don't think—"

"I do," he said. "I'm worried about Darin. I think he's in that state of mind. I'm not taking any chances."

"Look, Mr. Steele, Darin has lots of things to live

for. I don't think he's . . . you know, considering suicide, if that's what you're saying."

"That's what I'm saying." Mr. Steele went behind the bar and clinked ice cubes into his glass, the bar lights shining off his bald head. "Watch him closely for me, will you? If he talks about suicide, if he asks for your help—anything—tell me, OK?"

"Sure."

"And, Jeremy?"

"Yes?"

"Another favor?"

"Sure." I couldn't imagine what he was going to say next.

"This is difficult." He hesitated, scratching his chin. "Let me say first of all, I started Alcoholics Anonymous six weeks ago. Did you know that?"

"No, I didn't know. I mean, I noticed you've been drinking mineral water."

"It's taken me a long time to look at myself seriously. A dentist by day. A drunk by night. I've never been available when Darin needed me. I've always been absent because of the booze. I'd like to be here for him this time. His going to college, his not being able to fulfill all his dreams—this is going to be another crisis in his life. I want to be here this time. And . . . frankly, I want to save myself." He held up his ice-filled glass. "AA and mineral water, a splendid combination."

I was impressed but confused. "You wanted a favor?"

He set his glass on the bar. "I'd appreciate it if you wouldn't get him any more beer."

I felt my face turning red. "I, uh . . ."

"It's all right, Jeremy. At first I didn't mind. I figured, God, this kid's lost so much he has a right to some enjoyment in life, even if it isn't good for him. God knows he's seen me drink enough. The problem is, I think the beer increases his depression, makes him angrier, triggers more resentment. I'm really afraid of what he might try."

Mrs. Steele came into the room, and I stood up. "Of what who might try?" she said. "I thought I'd leave those two alone on the patio. Of what who might try?" she asked again.

"Nothing," Mr. Steele said, and poured his glass full of mineral water, the ice popping and cracking.

"Who were you talking about?" she insisted. "Were you talking about Darin?"

Mr. Steele stirred his drink with a swizzle stick. "If Darin tries to . . . to harm himself," Mr. Steele said, "if he starts talking about things like that, I want Jeremy to tell us."

Mrs. Steele waved off the thought. "Howard, are you harping about that again? He's in love. Haven't you two noticed? He's going to be perfectly fine, don't you think so, Jeremy?"

I drew in a deep breath. "I think you're right, Mrs. Steele." I gave them a half-wave. "See you. Tell Joy if she's going with me, I'll wait a minute."

"Poor Jeremy," Mrs. Steele said, "so patient and understanding. You're going to miss those two when you've gone off to the navy and they've gone to college together, aren't you?"

I nodded, then said, "Good night. Tell Joy I'll wait a minute."

Mrs. Steele's eyes flashed a smile at me. "I'll walk you to the door, Jeremy."

"No—no . . . That's all right. I know the way out."

Chapter
7

I STOOD IN FRONT OF DARIN'S HOUSE, THREW MY HEAD back, clenched my eyes shut, and breathed deeply, quickly, as if I'd sprinted a mile. The night was cooling off and turning damp with dew. I couldn't have stayed in that house another second without screaming: *Yes! I'm having lots of fun with your girl, Darin! Darin's losing Joy, too, Mr. Steele. We just haven't told you. I am not patient and understanding, Mrs. Steele! And leave me alone, will you?*

I opened my eyes. The moon had drifted away and only a scattering of stars remained. I stood there a moment, listening to the night sounds: traffic on the highway adjacent to the Sunnyside subdivision, the distant wail of a siren.

I looked at my watch. Eleven-thirty.

I'll wait one minute, Joy.

I walked down to the curb where my car was parked. I opened the door and slid in.

Darin, Joy, and I—our relationship started to seriously tangle last April when Joy said, "Let's all go to the prom together." We sat in Darin's van at Fairmont Cemetery. It was midnight, a cool spring night with tall pines hiding the moon. Six miles out of town in a wooded, hilly grove, the cemetery was a place where Joy, Darin, and I came to talk over problems and put things in order somehow; it was also the place where my dad was buried. I often wondered if he were watching and listening.

"That's crazy," I said. "Three people can't go to a dance together. I mean, not two guys and a girl."

"Yes, we can!" Joy was like that: full of off-the-wall ideas.

"Get a date," Darin said to me, and sipped his Bud. "You're ugly, but you should be able to find a stray dog."

"I don't even know a stray dog."

Joy said, "Listen, we've been going every place with each other since we were kids. Swimming pools, movies, concerts. None of us has been to the prom before. What do you say? Go with Darin and me?"

I shook my head. "No way."

"It's our last chance, the last school dance of our high school careers." Joy squeezed my arm. "Let's go."

"I don't like being a third wheel."

"Darin and I won't go without you," Joy said. "We'll all stay home."

"C'mon," Darin said. "Don't be a jerk. Joy's right. We've been every place else together. We want you with us."

"You want me along to be a chauffeur. Joy won't have to drive, and then you two can make out."

Darin grinned. "Hey, what are buddies for?"

"No thanks."

"Honestly," Darin said, "we really want you to come along. We've talked about it."

"Come on." Joy flicked my earlobe, stinging me.

"Ouch! Cut it out."

"Come on, Jeremy." Joy started to tickle my ribs. "I won't leave you alone," she said, laughing. "You want to be begged, don't you? I'm begging! *Please*, Jeremy."

She kept tickling me, and I started laughing, too. "What the hell, I'll go," I said. "I'll go. I'll drive. I'll be your chauffeur. I'll wait in the van till the dance is over."

"No, you guys each rent a tux. I'll buy a dress, and we'll all go together."

———

Joy's inviting me to the prom with Darin and her pleased me. Though we'd all been best friends since that summer we met at the swimming pool, I discovered in junior high that Darin had more than friendship in mind for Joy. That fact hit me hardest one summer afternoon when we went to a *Friday the Thirteenth* movie together. Joy and I were thirteen; Darin, fourteen. Joy sat between us. Because she was so frightened, we each held one of her hands. She squeezed my hand—I supposed Darin's, too— like crazy during the scary parts. During the middle of the movie, I spotted Darin's hand sneaking around the back of Joy's seat. Finally resting his arm on her shoulders, he let his hand dangle over her breast. I tried to watch his hand with one eye, the screen with the other; but as the bloody story unfolded on the screen, I lost concentration on Darin's hand.

Suddenly, Joy's hand crunched mine. I thought she was responding to what was happening on the screen. Glancing at her, I saw she was kissing Darin. And she was squeezing my hand harder! What the hell was going on? When her head sunk onto Darin's shoulder, I pried my fingers loose from her grip and stared at the screen. I watched Jason cut a guy's head off. I wished it were Darin's.

"You're not sore, are you?" Darin said after we'd walked Joy home from the movie.

"About what?" I said stiffly.

"About me making out with Joy."

"It's your business and hers," I said.

"Yeah, well, she likes me more than as just a friend. She has for a long time. I thought you should know in case you have any ideas about her."

"She's my friend. I don't have any ideas about her."

That last part was a lie. I'd had lots of ideas about Joy, all of them explicit. Now I felt betrayed. The rest of the summer I sulked like a baby. I tried to ignore Darin and Joy, refusing to go any place with them, even when Joy called and begged to make it a threesome.

In his sophomore and junior years, Darin was on the varsity football, wrestling, and track teams. Practicing took hours, and one season ran into the other. Joy always wanted someone to go with her to his games and meets. I was her choice. Ironically, I spent more time with her than Darin did because he was so busy. And I went to all her softball games.

I tried to summon the courage to challenge Darin for Joy. I ached to approach her. I invented endless scenarios in which I lured Joy away from him. My best plot was that I reminded her of our friendship and told her I needed a sexual experience before I went into the world alone. "What are friends for?" I'd ask her. "To take care of each other's needs," she'd reply. In my fantasy, once we made love, Joy found she liked me much more than Darin, and I became her man.

After Darin's accident, I dropped the idea of challenging him. Though I loved Joy, what was I going to do? Fight with my best friend over his girl—also my best friend? He was in a wheelchair. Joy was probably the only girl he'd ever find. For me, once I got initiated, there would be other girls. A sailor has a girl in every port, right?

Prom night changed everything.

The prom's theme was "Hold onto the Night." The colors were pink and black. Darin and I wore black tuxedos. At five-nine, Joy was statuesque in a pink silk formal sprinkled with sequins, her shoulders smooth and bare, a bit of cleavage showing. I had grown to six feet, still a bit skinny, but gone were the pimples, and contacts replaced glasses. My hair was short, chestnut-colored, and curly, like my mom's.

The dance was held in the Starlight Ballroom at the fairgrounds. Live music rocked the dance floor, guitars screaming, drums pounding, a singer wailing—the sounds so loud and feverish you had to scream to be heard. Lights whirled and flashed from the ceiling, spilling blue and orange, green and red across the dancers crowding the floor.

Joy and I showed Darin a wild time. We took turns pushing and spinning his chair around the floor for fast dances. During the slow ones we stood in corners, and I kept feeding him tiny sips of Jim Beam from a flask in my breast pocket. I wanted him to enjoy the moment, to hang on to the night. If a bit of alcohol would heighten the experience for him, so much the better. When would he have another chance to go crazy at a dance?

Near the end of the dance, Darin said, "God, you two are my best friends ever. I always knew it. Tonight is proof." He was holding Joy's hand, and I slipped the silver flask into his other hand. Darin jerked his head back and tilted the flask to his lips, his Adam's apple bobbing as he gulped.

"Hey, not so much. You won't last the night."

"That's enough," Joy said.

Darin stopped for breath. "To my best friends!" He wanted another hit, but I grabbed the flask from him, capped it, and slid it into my breast pocket.

"Save some for later," I said.

"Let's dance." Joy grabbed the handles on Darin's chair. "This is the last one."

"You two dance," Darin said. "This is a slow one. I don't like slow ones. Give me the flask."

"After the dance," I said. I took Joy's hand. "You want to?"

She smiled. "Sure."

I'd already danced a couple of fast ones with Joy, but not a slow one. I swallowed as she pressed against me, my arms circling her. Her blond hair flowed to her shoulders in soft curls; she smelled of flowers. My feet shuffled along clumsily, trying to follow hers. "Relax," she whispered, her breath warm in my ear.

"I'm trying."

When we had worked our way across the floor, out of Darin's sight, our feet gradually stopped moving. We simply stood, swaying in rhythm to the music, her arms looped around my neck, her head on my shoulder, her soft hair against my cheek.

"We've never danced like this before," I said, hoarsely.

"I know. It's a shame. All these years."

Suddenly I felt a secret intimacy between us, like a flash of fire, feeding on itself, getting hotter and hotter. As the final sounds of the music drifted away, she pressed against me tighter and kissed me quickly, sweetly, on the lips. My head whirled.

When we got back to Darin, his head was starting to flop when he talked, a sign he was wasted, getting ready to pass out. "You guys dance." He was slurring his words. "Dance anytime you want. You are my very best friends ever. . . . Dance . . ."

I didn't think I'd fed him that much Jim Beam, but I didn't know what he might have had at home—I knew his parents let him drink a little beer. By the time Joy and I wheeled him off the dance floor and loaded him into his van, he was passed out.

"What'll we do with him?" I asked, sorry that I'd let him drink so much, feeling guilty.

"Take him home." Joy sat in the captain's chair next to the driver's.

"What about the party?"

After the dance, everyone was supposed to attend the after-prom party at Northpark Mall; it started at midnight and lasted till 5:00 A.M. The idea of the party was to keep all of us kids locked in the mall for a Las Vegas night, during which we gambled with play money. At the end of the party, we could buy prizes with our winnings, some really great stuff: a compact disk player, portable color TV, Walkman radio, electric typewriter. The organizers—administrators, parents, teachers—hoped that by the time they let us go at five, we'd be too tired to drink, drive, and get into trouble.

"We can't take him to the party," Joy said. "Everyone will know for sure he's been drinking. He'll get kicked out—I'll get kicked out. We'll all be in trouble. I could get the boot from the softball team."

Joy was right. She and Darin had downed two beers in Darin's van before going into the prom. I didn't have any; I was driving.

We delivered Darin to his parents and apologized sheepishly for his condition, explaining that we were only trying to make sure he had a good time. A little drunk, Mr. Steele smiled and said he understood and thanked us for having the good sense to bring Darin home. Mrs. Steele was miffed. "You two have ruined Darin's evening." She said it with her eyes hard on Joy, as if holding Joy responsible. Then she said to me, "I hope you'll take Joy straight home." I thought she was reminding me that Joy was Darin's girl.

We escaped the house as quickly as possible, Mrs. Steele scowling at us all the way. We sat a moment in my car parked in front of Darin's house, watching all the lights go out, except in Darin's bedroom. His parents had to help dress and undress him every day.

"The accident should've never happened," Joy said quietly.

I was surprised she said that—she never ever talked about the accident; neither did Darin. I supposed the memory was too painful for both of them. I hadn't questioned Joy about the accident since the night it happened. I didn't know why Darin had dove into the shallow end of the pool, breaking his neck. I assumed he'd been drinking. I'd asked Darin only once about the details. His reply was simple: "I don't want to talk about it." I hoped someday Joy would trust me enough to tell me what had happened without being asked. I had too much respect and love for her to try to drag the story out of her at that moment, so I changed the subject.

"I don't think Mrs. Steele trusts us together," I said.

"Probably not."

"Should we hit the after-prom party?"

"Do you want to?"

I looked at her and remembered how she'd kissed me on the dance floor. My lips ached for another kiss like that, and I wanted desperately to let her know how much I cared for her, how I thought about her all the time, how I fantasized about her.

I took a silent breath. "There's part of a twelve-pack left in the cooler. You want to park in the cemetery?"

She looked at me, surprised, I think. "I'd like that," she said.

We parked in the cemetery next to towering pines silhouetted against a moonlit sky. To our right, tombstones dotted a hillside, looking as if they were chiseled from ink-black granite.

Are you watching, Dad? Are you listening?

"So what's going to happen to us after this summer?" I said.

Joy shrugged. "Darin and I will be off to college and you'll be in the navy. It's sad to think about us parting."

"Do you suppose we'll always be friends, the three of us?"

"I think so," she said. "Always."

She smiled at me, and I gained courage. "Do you love Darin? Do you really want to go to Iowa with him?"

She leaned against her door. "I don't know. He wants me to go pretty bad. A lot depends on the softball season, if I get a scholarship or not."

"Do you love him?"

She thought a moment. "Can I give you an honest answer? One you won't repeat."

"Yes."

"I have great feelings for Darin." She spoke in a quiet voice, oddly soft. "But I don't love him the way he wants me to."

"But you're going to remain his girlfriend."

"Yes."

"Because of loyalty?"

She stared through the windshield. "Yes. I owe him that."

"Why?"

She didn't answer.

"Have you ever thought that if Darin really loved you, he'd let you go?"

"I have to stay with him."

"Why?" I asked again.

Again she didn't answer, and she still wouldn't look at me. Suddenly the car was getting warm inside. Maybe it was just me. Or the tux I was wearing. I pulled off the bow tie and unbuttoned the collar. I rolled down my window and cool night air rushed in, carrying the chirp of crickets. "Can I ask you something else?"

"What?"

"Are you and Darin . . . ?"

"What?" I think she knew what I was going to ask.

I hesitated. I didn't want to offend her, and it was none of my business anyway. "Never mind."

"What?"

"Forget it."

"No," she said in that same oddly quiet voice. "Darin and I aren't making it. Is that what you wanted to know?"

"Yes."

"We never have. He wanted to all the time, and we . . ." Though her voice trailed off, I thought she was going to continue with an explanation of why they hadn't, but all she added was, "We didn't . . . we just didn't, that's all."

"He probably couldn't do it now, could he? I mean, like he is?"

"I don't think so, but I don't know. I mean, his operation in January did him a lot of good." She shrugged. "They think he'll walk someday. Anything is possible."

Popping open two cans of beer, I handed Joy one, took a deep swallow of mine, and made a face as it burned a path down my throat to my stomach. Sitting alone with her in the car and drinking a beer gave me such a rush, stirred my feelings so deeply,

I couldn't keep my mouth shut. "I . . . I like you a lot," I said abruptly. "I . . . always have."

She smiled: "I know."

"You do?"

"Yes."

"I mean more than as just a friend."

"I know that, too."

"I've wanted to tell you for a couple of years. Would you believe it?"

"Yes."

Taking another swallow of beer, I waited for her to say she liked me, but she didn't. "Look," I said, deciding to move on. "You know, I've hardly dated anyone. I've, uh, never done it. I guess neither have you, and so we're going to be out in the real world, not knowing anything, you in college, me in the navy."

She was looking at me intently.

"Do you know what it's going to be like, being so stupid about things? How scary it's going to be? Do you have any idea?"

"I think so," she said.

I stared at her, hardly able to believe I was actually saying this. I mean, friends ask one another for help and advice, but this—was this too much to ask of a friend? As my blood pumped faster and faster, I said, "I . . . I don't want to have sex for the first time with a stranger."

Joy sipped her beer and regarded me solemnly. "Me, neither."

I took another swallow of mine. "If you and Darin were already making love, I wouldn't mention this. That would be like asking you to be unfaithful. Like committing adultery. Do you understand what I'm trying to say?"

"Yes."

"You're sure you and Darin aren't?"

"Yes."

"We wouldn't fall in love or anything like that," I said.

"Of course not."

"We'd do it just for the experience."

"Right," she said.

"For the fun."

She nodded.

"We wouldn't be hurting anyone," I said. "Darin will never know."

"We'd never ever tell him," she said.

Despite the cold beer, my mouth was suddenly dry and my knees were trembling. And suddenly my bravado vanished. I was scared. Suddenly I was hoping she'd say something like, "Get serious, Jeremy!" But she wasn't saying anything like that, and now she was no longer regarding me solemnly. Instead, a smile flickered across her face: this was the kind of far-out idea she liked.

"You're positive you and Darin aren't?" My palms felt moist.

Joy's smile grew wider; she knew I was chickening out. "Jeremy, I should know if Darin and I are making love."

"I know, but—"

"Jeremy, it's all right."

"Maybe we should forget it."

"No," she said. "I don't think so."

"It wouldn't be right."

"Jeremy, I like you, too," Joy said softly. She touched my hand with cool fingers and leaned toward me. "I have for a long, long time."

We kissed, my heart beating wildly. Then I took a big swallow of beer and didn't taste it. "We'll never tell Darin," I said again. "He's our best friend."

Joy set her beer on the floor, then looked directly at me. "The best of friends have secrets, Jeremy. Believe me."

She unzipped the back of her formal. Following her lead, I unbuttoned my shirt but started trembling. *What was she going to do with her formal? Slip it down to her waist? What was she wearing under it?*

"Do you have something?" she said.

"You mean like a disease?" I was staring at her, wondering if there would be enough room in the car.

I couldn't stop shaking.

Start the car, Jeremy. Take her home.

Joy laughed. "No, Jeremy, do you have a condom?"

I shook my head. "Maybe we should wait. . . ."

"That's all right, but you'll have to withdraw."

"Withdraw?" I heard the sound of my own ragged breathing.

"Pull out early," she said, and laughed.

"Stop laughing."

"You said we could laugh." She was still laughing.

We made love in the hot, cramped backseat of the car, her formal and my tux crumpled on the floor in the front seat. When the pull-out time came, I was too excited, too blown away to remember.

Chapter

8

JOY'S OPENING THE CAR DOOR STARTLED ME BACK TO the present.

"I'm glad you waited," she said, and climbed into the car. "I'm so tired I can hardly stand."

It was nearly midnight. I'd rolled the windows down on both sides of the car, letting the cool night air circulate.

"I was going to wait a minute. Not a half-hour."

She kissed me on the cheek.

The thought that a moment ago her lips had been kissing Darin's made me sick. I pulled away from her.

"What's wrong?" she said.

"What took you so long? Is Darin looking for more than kisses? He's got two good hands."

She looked at me sharply. "Jeremy, don't talk like that!"

"Well, what do you expect? He makes me so mad lately. Why do we put up with him?"

"He's a friend. We can't give up on him. Look, would you give up on a person who has cancer? My grandmother had Alzheimer's. My family didn't give up on her. We still loved her."

"I know, but—" Frustrated, I pounded the steering wheel, accidently sounding the horn.

"Jeremy, let's go home. We're going to wake up the neighborhood."

Joy was right: we couldn't give up on Darin. I twisted the key in the ignition. The Buick clicked to life, and I pulled away from the curb.

"Mr. Steele is worried about Darin," I said. "He thinks Darin's depressed. Do you think Darin's depressed?"

"I don't know," she said. "He's moody. Sometimes he talks about walking again and driving a car and swimming. Even playing football. Then sometimes he doesn't care about anything, doesn't care what he says to anybody. He was in a bad mood tonight."

"I made things worse: I let him have too many beers, but I was tired of listening to him complain. He didn't complain when you started kissing him in the back of the van, though."

"Jeremy, *don't!*"

"I'm sorry," I said. We fell silent once more. I turned left onto the highway and watched my headlights follow the center line headed toward Maple Grove. "Mr. Steele is going to AA. Did you know that?"

"Alcoholics Anonymous?" Joy said.

"Yes."

"Who told you that?"

"He did. Tonight."

"I wondered why I hadn't seen him drinking lately. Good for him. I wonder why Darin didn't mention it."

"Mr. Steele doesn't want me to let Darin have any more beer," I said. "He thinks when Darin drinks too much he sinks into his down moods. He thinks Darin might do something stupid."

"Suicide?"

I nodded. "Mr. Steele's put all the pills and knives in the house out of Darin's reach."

That forced us into another silence, Joy sitting rigid in her seat, looking straight ahead. Then she said, "No matter what happens, Jeremy, we can't ever tell him about us. We can't do that to him. Remember what we said?"

"I know."

"Not ever. He's going through something we can't even imagine."

"All right. I understand that, but it kills me to hear him yell at you, to see him demand your kisses as if you owe him something. It might not be long and he'll be demanding more."

Joy didn't answer.

When we arrived at Maple Grove, there was hardly any traffic on the streets. High school kids who nightly cruised Main Street and the town square during the summer were probably partying, celebrating the Leafs' win.

"I wish I'd been quicker and smarter in junior high," I said, "but Darin made his move first."

Joy smiled. "You were never going to make a move, Jeremy. You were still so shy, so bashful then."

"And Darin turned out to be a high school football star on the varsity as a sophomore. A stud. That impressed you, didn't it?"

"I admit it. I was thrilled that he liked me. Lots of high school girls liked him, but he liked me—a ninth-grader. And he has always been fun to be with. It's only the last couple of months he's been so moody, so difficult to get along with."

"The night of the prom is the last time I can remember him having fun."

"He really wanted you to come with us. He didn't want you sitting home by yourself. He was thinking about you, and look what it got him."

"What's that mean?"

"We betrayed him."

Joy lived in an older but well-kept part of town with two-story houses, sprawling lawns, and ancient trees. As I made a right turn, my car lights cut a path down her tree-lined street, and I felt her gaze on the side of my face.

"I think he knows about us," she said.

I shook my head. "I don't think so."

"You heard what he said to you tonight."

"It's paranoia. Depression breeds paranoia. He doesn't know anything."

"He says things to me, too: 'Do you kiss Jeremy when I'm not around?' He suspects and can't do anything about it. We're the ones who are making him depressed."

I shook my head again. "His father thinks he's depressed because he won't be able to play football when he goes to college."

"Maybe that's a small part of it. . . . Listen, how would you feel if you thought your girlfriend was making out with your best friend?"

"I'd punch the guy out, I guess."

"Well, Darin can only yell and scream and pound the arms of his chair. Being in a chair and not being able to do what he wants is frustrating enough. Now he's wondering about us. He can't help being depressed."

I flexed my fingers on the steering wheel.

Was she right?

I felt her gaze again. "What are you thinking now?"

"I think we should stop, Jeremy." She said it softly, firmly.

I nearly veered into a parked car.

"Watch where you're going."

I looked straight ahead. "You don't really mean that," I said carefully, and pulled in front of Joy's house, stopping under an oak tree. The glow of a streetlight at the corner filtered through the leaves.

She leaned against her door. "Yes, I mean it. Stop."

"You're serious?"

"Yes."

"I can't believe it. I mean, I admit things are a little bumpy right now, but . . ."

"Jeremy, it's been a beautiful spring and summer. If it doesn't turn out exactly the way we planned, so what? We'll survive. We'll always remember. Besides, I can't be two people any longer: one making love with you, the other being Darin's girlfriend. It's too hard."

I turned the key, shutting down the engine, and turned out the headlights. Sliding toward Joy, I took her hands in mine. "You know what I thought in the beginning?" I asked. "A summer of sex between two friends, what can it hurt? It'll be fun. I admit I thought only about the excitement. I didn't think about how I'd hurt inside later, watching you with Darin. I mean, I'd seen him kiss you hundreds of times before, but it's different now. At least I react differently." I shook my head. "I'm two people, too: Darin's friend and his rival. Maybe it was a bad, bad idea."

"Jeremy, it wasn't a bad idea. I have a wonderful scrapbook in my mind: you and me in the cemetery that first time—how scared we were because we didn't use a condom and you didn't pull out."

"We got lucky," I said. "No condom—I'd never do that again."

"Me, neither." Then Joy smiled. "There were two times at my house, one in your mother's cooler at the tavern—and on the pool table."

I laughed, too. "God, nobody would believe it."

"They don't write books like this," she said.

"I don't want any of us to get hurt." I squeezed her hands. "But I'm hurting already. I'm in love with you, Joy."

Her eyebrows jumped, and she jerked her hands away. "You can't be! We said we weren't going to fall in love. We can't!"

"What if it's already happened?"

"Dumb question, Jeremy. We have to stop, that's all."

"I'm not sure I can."

"No, no, Jeremy! We have no future. You already said you're hurting. I'm hurting, and we're hurting Darin."

"We have our own lives, Joy."

"Don't you see? Darin can't help being the way he is, and he's going to get a lot better. Mentally and physically. We can't do anything else that might hurt him or ruin his recovery. At least I can't." Tears hovered on her eyelashes. "It's over, Jeremy."

I fastened my eyes on her. "All right, if you think that's the way it should be, we'll stop. Just like that. *Wham!* Stop! I can do it. You know how many times we've done it? Twelve. That's enough experience. That's it! We're history."

"Oh, Jeremy." Joy's tears suddenly burst out of her eyes, tumbling down her cheeks. She lunged into my arms. "I don't want to lose what we have, but our lives are getting so complicated. If we're not careful, if Darin really finds out everything we've been doing, we'll destroy him."

"*Shhh.*" I stroked her hair and felt her hot tears on my shoulder through my T-shirt. A lump grew in my throat. "Look, Joy, I've got an idea." I held her by the shoulders at arm's length.

"What?"

"Let's say we put everything on hold till after the state tournament."

"On hold?"

"On hold." I lifted her chin with the crook of my forefinger. "What I'm saying is, we'll cool it so you can put all your energy, your time, your concentration on winning the state tournament. Make that priority one. After that we'll sit down and decide what to do about Darin and us. Let's not make hasty decisions right now. What do you think?"

She was beginning to hiccup. "We have to stop. You'll be leaving for the navy in September anyway."

"Listen to me. Put all of this out of your mind. Think nothing but softball." I stroked her hair. "After the tourney we'll untangle this mess we're in. OK?"

She kept hiccuping. "All right."

"Hold your breath." I patted her back, hoping to stop her hiccups. After a moment, she looked up at me, still holding her breath. I waited a few moments longer. When she let out her breath, I kissed her.

"What about tonight?" she said, her voice husky. "Are we on hold?"

"What do you think?" I said. "It's up to you. Whatever you want."

"We shouldn't," she said, and hiccuped again.

My heart sank. "All right," I said. "Whatever you say."

Chapter

9

"YOU'RE LATE TONIGHT," MOM SAID AS I WALKED IN through the back door of the tavern. Mom was behind the bar washing mugs. The place was empty because she serves an older crowd—mostly retired farmers and John Deere workers—and on weeknights they give up early. Cigarette and cigar smoke hung heavy in the air, creating a haze around the neon beer signs, and the place smelled of stale beer. That's why I seldom drank it: I hated the smell.

Mom was wearing jeans and a T-shirt. Half-moon silver earrings dangled from her ears, streaks of gray creeping into her short curly hair. In her younger days she had been an exotic dancer—I'd never told anyone at school that—and had met Dad when she was working in Des Moines. He had been a beer-truck driver; they got married and bought this little place in Maple Grove in the middle of town.

A gunman killed Dad during a robbery when I was six. Dad tried to shoot it out with the guy and died behind the bar, two bullets in his chest. We lived upstairs above the tavern. Mom heard the shots, ran down the inside stairs, which open in back by the walk-in cooler. She swung the stairway door open, a .22 pistol in her hands. She was too late. The gunman was gone; he was never caught. Mom's run the tavern since Dad died.

"Where have you been?" Mom added two more mugs to the row on the bar. "The game must've been over eight or nine hours ago. I saw on TV we won."

"Mom, I'm eighteen—not fifteen."

"But I still worry about where you are, how much sleep you're *not* getting."

Mom always worried about my not getting enough sleep. I cleaned the tavern for her every night—swept and mopped—and restocked the coolers. I waxed and buffed the floor after Sunday night's customers left. Mom paid me a good wage, more than I deserved. I also delivered the *Riverbend Times* in the morning, ninety-seven customers daily, 150 on Sunday. I usually finished cleaning the tavern anywhere from 1:00 to 3:00 A.M. Usually by three, the *Times* bundle-drop driver tossed my papers on the sidewalk in front of the Uptown. I'd finish delivering between 4:00 and 5:00 A.M., fall into bed, and sleep till nine or ten. That's why Mom worried about how much sleep I wasn't getting. I'd been delivering papers and cleaning the tavern since I was a junior in high school. Then I got even less sleep because I had to be in class by 8:00 A.M. I slept a lot in the afternoon.

"It was a long game," I said. "Lots of walks. After the ride back, we had to stop at Darin's house."

"Naturally." Though Mom had never said so, I suspected she didn't like Darin very much, but she liked Joy a lot.

"Then I took Joy home." I started picking up the ashtrays from the tables and putting them on the bar.

"How long did that take?" Mom smiled. I think she knew I liked Joy. A couple of times I'd brought Joy with me to help clean the tavern and the job had taken longer than usual. Mom could always tell when I finished because she could hear me locking up to leave and deliver my route.

"Not long."

"You're going to miss her, aren't you?"

"A little, I guess." Finished with the ashtrays, I started hoisting the bar stools onto the bar, setting them upside down on their cushioned seats.

"I don't know why you did that, drove off to Des Moines, took your physical, and enlisted—and not even telling me. It was your birthday!"

"Mom, we talked about it lots of times before. You even said it was OK if I joined the navy."

"Jeremy, you didn't say anything to me the day you left to sign up. You just—left."

"I knew you'd keep trying to talk me out of joining. You didn't mean it when you said it was OK. You just wanted me to stop talking about it."

"You should have given it more thought."

I set the last of the twelve stools on the bar. "Mom, I've told you: there's nothing to do in this town unless you want to work for John Deere. I don't. I can't afford to go to college like Darin; I didn't earn a scholarship like Joy probably will."

"You could go to junior college in Riverbend."

"And live in Maple Grove? Cruise the loop with the high school kids? Hang out at the Mac Shack? I don't think so. Besides, the navy will send me to its best electronic schools. I might get on a nuclear sub."

"Great, just great, Jeremy. Every mother wants her only child sailing around the bottom of the ocean." Mom opened the freezer behind the bar and started clinking mugs in so they'd be frosty tomorrow.

I didn't know: maybe I was wrong joining the navy, leaving Mom alone. The only family Mom and I had was each other. I'd never had a grandma or grandpa, or aunts and uncles, or cousins to hang around with. Mom came from Pennsylvania; she left home when she was eighteen. Dad was born in

Oregon. They never went back to their hometowns or called or wrote to any family that I know of. I think Mom was afraid that once I left for the navy she'd never see me again, as her own parents had never seen her again.

I started carrying the tables into the far corner by the window.

"What do Darin and Joy think of your leaving?" Mom said.

"What's there to think about? We know we can't hang around together forever. At least not all three of us."

"That means Darin and Joy will be together?"

"They'll probably go to college together. I don't know what'll happen after that."

"I still remember that first afternoon you brought them here for pop and candy."

"Me, too. Nine years ago."

"That's a long time," Mom said. "I didn't even know your father that long."

"What were my grandparents like?" I asked abruptly. I asked questions like that whenever I found the opportunity.

Mom pursed her lips. "Someday, Jeremy, I'm going to tell you all about them."

"You always say that."

"I mean it, I really will."

"When?"

"When the time's right and you're old enough to understand."

"I'm old enough to handle whatever you have to tell me," I said. "Joy and Darin, they've got pictures all around their houses of relatives. We don't."

"I know."

"What's the big deal? What's the secret?"

"Be patient."

Disgusted and tired, I said, "Forget it" and headed for the back room, where I kept the broom.

Mom often brought out mixed feelings in me. I loved her, but when I was younger I felt she'd cheated me because I didn't have a father. She should have married someone who wasn't a tavern owner and who wouldn't have been shot. She should have been a teacher like Joy's mother. I should have lived in a house, not above a tavern, with a mother *and* a father, like most of the kids I went to school with.

I thought the differences in my life showed, as if I were wearing a sign advertising them, so I was shy. Before I met Darin and Joy, I didn't hang around with anyone. I read all the time, even as a little kid. Gradually Darin and Joy changed me. I got interested in sports, though I never played. From Darin I learned to be brash and assertive; from Joy, impulsive and fun loving. Best friends can do a lot for a person.

When I came back and started sweeping near the

front door, Mom said, "Look, I'm beat. I'm going up to bed. You've had a long day, too. Just sweep if you want to."

"No, I'll mop. The place should sparkle every morning."

Mom smiled. "You're a good son, Jeremy. I don't know what I'll do without you."

Chapter

10

After cleaning the tavern and delivering my route, I collapsed into bed. I woke in the morning at nine, exhausted, excited, and worried. I was excited that the Maple Leafs had a chance to win the state softball tournament. What a boost to this nothing little prairie town in eastern Iowa, population four thousand. Coach Thorton had won the Class-A football title three years ago, but that was the only state title the school had won in the last decade. Softball, volleyball, basketball, track, swimming—our girls had never won a state title. Of course, I was worried about Joy. Could she put her tangled relationship with Darin and me out of her mind for a week and pitch winning softball? I hoped so. And

I was worried about Joy and me. Did we have a future together without destroying Darin? What a mess.

When I got up, Mom was gone. She always left after breakfast to buy liquor and/or do her banking. She never kept much liquor or cash on hand. Why let a thief break in and steal it?

I showered, dressed, and ate a bowl of cereal and milk. Our place above the tavern wasn't bad; it was roomy, airy, and comfortable, with a big living room, kitchen, pantry, two bedrooms—all the rooms carpeted and nicely painted, colorful curtains hanging from the windows. It wasn't a house, though.

Sitting at the computer in my room, I updated the team's stats (I also kept Mom's books on the computer) and printed a copy of the stats for Coach Thorton. Notable among the stats was Shawna Lucas's .467 batting average, Corky Robinson's 35 RBIs and 10 home runs, and Joy's .75 ERA. The team batting average was .320.

Creaky, dark stairs from the kitchen led downstairs to the tavern. When I came down, Hazel, Mom's daytime bartender, was behind the bar using the remote control to adjust the TV; it sat high in a corner on a chain-suspended platform hanging from the ceiling.

"Morning, Hazel." I pulled out a stool and sat at the end of the bar by the TV. "Where's the morning paper?"

"Hold your horses," she said, and kept flipping through the TV stations with the remote control. Ornery, hard working, probably sixty, Hazel opened at seven every morning and worked till four, when Mom took over. If either Mom or Hazel was sick or needed time off, Mom hired one of her patrons to take over. The Uptown was truly a small-town bar.

"Where's the paper?" I asked.

"I'm not even sure the kid left it this morning."

"Right. How could I miss delivering here?"

"Well, it happens, you know. Every time you're short papers who doesn't get one? Then I miss the coupons."

"Give me a break, Hazel. I left one by the register, where I always leave it."

Hazel reached down by the glasses, then slapped the paper on the bar. "I seen on TV last night your girlfriend won."

"She's not my girlfriend. Just a friend. Thanks for the paper."

I turned immediately to the sports page. I usually read the paper before I went to bed, but this morning I'd been too tired.

LEAFS ADVANCE TO FINALS
KELLEY KILLS CENTERVILLE

By Jim Kelley, Sports Editor

Maple Leaf pitcher Joy Kelley mowed down ten Centerville batters with strikeouts Wednesday as the Leafs won the Centerville Regional softball title 2–1 advanced to the championship round of the state tournament.

The finals are scheduled to open Monday at Riverbend Public School Park with the title game slated for Friday at 7:30 P.M.

Kelley was spectacular as she gave up only three hits over seven innings, overpowering Centerville hitters. . . .

I skimmed through the rest of the story, noting with a smile that Mr. Kelley mentioned Joy's ten walks only in passing. What I really wanted to know was what other teams had made it to the sixteen-team field, and who would Maple Grove play first? Mr. Kelley concluded his story saying the Iowa Softball Association would announce tournament pairings later in the week.

I drove over to the girls' practice field adjacent to the school. The morning was cool, sunny, and breezy, with blue skies—a beautiful day for July.

It was ten when I parked next to school and

walked across the grassy field to the girls' diamond, stat sheet for Coach Thorton in an envelope. Practice nearly over, the team sat in center field in a circle surrounding Thorton. It was lecture/pep-talk time. A disciplinarian, Thorton's real sport was football. He turned out burly, hit-'em-hard teams on defense, but his offense showed little imagination. The school board dumped the softball job on him when the former coach had quit teaching two years ago and the board couldn't find anyone else to replace him. Thorton had had to learn softball from scratch, but a team of talented, determined upperclassmen and Joy's pitching had carried him along.

A few parents sat in bleachers along the first-base line, and I leaned on the left-field fence. We all listened: "There's no reason why we can't win this thing," Thorton was saying. Some of the girls leaned back on their hands; others sat cross-legged, heads down, pulling at the grass. All of them wore T-shirts and sweatpants. "We've got an experienced, senior-dominated team, a lot of leadership here. Most of you girls have been playing together since grade school. You know what it means to play as a team, to sacrifice personal glory for the team. You know what it means to win. Now I'm going to show you how it feels to win the big ones, nothing less than the state championship. We're not happy just to be in the finals. We want it all! The title! The trophy!

The glory! We're going to kick *ass!*" He started shaking his finger at the circle of girls, pivoting as he did so. "But each one of you has got to want it so bad, so hard, that the thought of winning consumes you. Nothing else matters this week. *WIN* is the word! Every muscle in your body is tuned to that one word. *WIN!*"

Joy was one of the girls leaning back on her hands. I thought she was looking at me, so I gave a little wave. But she didn't see me. She suddenly plopped back flat on the grass, her forearm over her eyes.

"We had a lousy practice today," Thorton went on. "I told you to stay away from parties last night, but half of you stagger in here this morning with hangovers, your asses dragging. Pardon me, ladies, but it's the truth. If you can't run to first base, stoop to pick up a ground ball, or see the ball to hit, what kind of practice can we have?"

Some of the girls started to squirm under Thorton's fire. Most parents were standing up in the bleachers now. Thorton knew he'd better back off. Yelling and screaming too long wouldn't do anything but hurt the girls' feelings and tick off the parents, a bad combination if he planned on winning the state title.

"So look!" he continued. "What I'm telling you is, we've got three days left for good practices. That's plenty. We need to keep mentally sharp, work on execution, and concentrate on winning. I want you to go home, relax, eat good, and get to bed by ten o'clock. Don't be surprised if I call for a bed check." He clapped his hands. "Up! Five laps around the field! Let's go!"

The team groaned, most of the girls slowly dragging themselves to their feet. Joy remained flat on her back on the grass. Thorton bent over her, pulling her arm off her face. She sat up, forearms on her knees, head hanging as Thorton talked to her. She nodded a couple of times, then got up and jogged far behind the other girls.

Cupping his hands around his mouth, Thorton yelled, "Pick it up! For future state champs, you girls run like cows!" He turned and came striding across the outfield toward me. His face looked like stone. He stopped at the fence, and I handed him the envelope. "The team's batting .320," I said. "That's not bad."

He nodded, stared at the envelope a moment, then looked at me. "You know, Jeremy, to be a successful coach these days you have to be part parent, part doctor, part psychiatrist. It's not easy, and coaching girls isn't exactly my thing." He seemed to be making an extra effort to keep his voice down.

"I understand." I shuffled my feet and suddenly felt uneasy.

Why is he telling me this?

"Jeremy, you do a lot for the team, keeping these stats for us just because you like to. I appreciate that."

"Thanks."

Little beads of sweat glistened above his lip. "But I thought you'd know better than to take Joy partying last night."

I was stunned. "What?"

"Partying! Lucas had a hangover. Robinson, too—"

"Joy didn't party last night."

"I think it's great the way you and Joy have remained loyal to Darin Steele, the way you two take him everywhere in his van. But I hold you responsible, Jeremy. From what I see, you drive Darin's van all the time. You're the leader here. You have access to the booze from your mother's tavern."

"Wait a minute—"

He cut me off. "If you're going to take Joy out drinking you can at *least* wait till the tournament is over. Winning the regional title is nothing. We want state. Then you guys can party."

I was getting hot. "Joy didn't party last night."

"Don't lie to me, Jeremy. I'm trying to be calm about this. I'm trying to reason with you."

"I'm not lying."

Thorton looked across the field at the batting net set up along the right-field line. Then he looked back at me. "Then you tell me why she started throwing up when she took batting practice. Tell me why she spent nearly the whole morning in the dugout heaving her guts out into a bucket."

"Heaving?"

"Practically the whole morning. You tell me why."

I swallowed. "Did she say she was partying?"

"I asked her, and she didn't deny it. What do you think I am, stupid? I can tell." He shook his head. "Look, I know she's Darin's girl. I don't know how much influence you have in her life, but if you take her out partying again this week, if she shows up again at practice throwing up, I'm going to have a talk with her parents. And your mother. Do you understand?"

"Yes."

"If somehow this thing is Darin Steele's fault, then you make sure he gets the message. Do you hear?"

"Yes, sir."

"I got no choice. I like Darin. I like you. I like Joy. She's a hell of an athlete. You're a great kid. Darin's a tragic case. But I can't let Joy get screwed up. This team needs her. Do you understand what I'm saying?"

"I do," I said. "I won't let it happen again."

He walked away.

I was mad as hell. I knew what had happened. After I'd taken Joy home, Darin had called her and convinced her to come back and pick him up at his house. She'd sneaked him out and they'd gone partying. She was trying to dump me so she could spend more time with him.

Jealousy bit a chunk out of my heart.

It was nearly eleven; the sun was starting to burn.

Breathing hard, Joy reached the fence and leaned on it, her arms crossed at the top. She looked ashen, strands of blond hair matted to her face with sweat.

Out partying all night—heaving in a bucket all morning served her right.

"You don't look so good." I leaned on the fence, too.

"It's nothing," she said.

"You look worse than you did yesterday after seven innings."

"Thanks a lot, Jeremy."

"You going home to shower and change before you go to work?"

She nodded. "I have to be in at noon. What time is it?"

I glanced at my wristwatch. "Nearly eleven. You feel good enough to work?"

"I'm all right."

I put the palm of my hand to her forehead. "You're sweating, but you feel chilled."

"It's the flu or something."

"Are you really going to work?"

"Yes."

"Meet me at the square before you go in, OK?"

Joy shielded her eyes from the sun with her hand and looked at me. "Is it about what we decided last night? You're changing your mind about putting us on hold."

I shook my head. "No," I said, "it's not that. It's about your getting me into trouble with Coach Thorton." I stepped back from the fence. "See you later."

Chapter
11

Joy and I sat on a park bench in the Maple Grove town square. The square was actually a huge, beautifully kept park in the middle of town, tall maples shading green grass and rock gardens of marigolds, petunias, and daisies. A twelve-foot-tall bronze statue of Chief Blackhawk stood in the middle of the park. Across the street on all four sides, Maple Grove businesses surrounded the square—the bank, the theater, and the Uptown Tavern. Joy worked at From the Heart craft shop and had to go to work in a few minutes.

I'd been waiting for her at least a half-hour. "I want to know what's going on," I said.

"Nothing." She wore a blue blouse, denim miniskirt, and white sandals, no socks, her hair swept back tight to her skull and braided into a single pigtail with a blue ribbon tied at the end. She still looked peaked, but she had covered the look with delicate touches of eyeliner, mascara, and lip gloss.

"Thorton said half of the girls had hangovers," I said.

"Lucas and Robinson, they were the only ones. You know how excitable he is, how he blows everything out of proportion."

"He accused me of taking you partying last night."

She turned away.

"He sounded as if you admitted you were partying. Did you drive back to Darin's last night and take him out?"

"What gave you that stupid idea?"

"Did you?"

"No! You heard his parents say he had to go to bed."

"Did you let Thorton think you had a hangover?" I asked.

"Yes . . ."

"Why? He chewed me out, as if the hangover were my fault."

She sighed heavily. "Because I didn't feel good this morning, that's why. I wanted him to leave me alone. He can believe whatever he wants to believe. I've got too many other problems—you and Darin, for example—to worry about what he thinks."

"Thorton said you spent nearly all morning in the dugout, throwing up into a bucket."

"He told you that?"

"Yes."

We sat in silence as I waited for an explanation. Cars moved slowly around the square, drivers looking for a place to park. A soft breeze blew, helping cool the shade under the maples. Blue jays, robins, and squirrels played in the park.

"Maybe it was that half-warm Big Mac you fed me last night," Joy said. "Sometimes people just get sick, that's all. I happened to be sick this morning. Maybe it's the flu."

I let it go.

I said, "How about if I pick you up from work this afternoon. We'll work on pitching mechanics—stance, windup, and release. Maybe we can eliminate some of your wildness. In this heat too many pitches tire you out too fast."

"I'm not that wild."

"Ten walks last game. Eight in the previous game. You were averaging only seven a game before that."

The shrill noonday whistle blasted from the Maple Grove fire station two blocks away. It startled both of us, and we jumped. Brown paper bags in hand, clerks poured out of the stores. They walked hurriedly across the street toward the square, where they'd sit on benches, picnic tables, or the grass to eat their lunches.

Though I'd never played softball, I knew what I was talking about when I said Joy's working on mechanics might help her wildness. School library, public library, sporting goods stores—I'd borrowed and bought and read every book about softball I could get my hands on. I'd bet I'd seen more softball games and practices than Coach Thorton had. And Joy listened. That's one thing about her: When it came to softball, she listened; she was coachable.

"Jeremy, I have to go now."

"When you get off work, OK?"

"We shouldn't spend too much time together. We should avoid temptation."

"We're going to talk softball. Five o'clock, OK?"

"All right."

I watched Joy walk slowly across the street. She usually sprinted to wherever she was going. Now she trudged along as if she had lead in her sandals.

Definitely, something was wrong with her.

Maybe it was the flu. Serious cases of the flu put people flat on their backs in bed. Could a virus end Maple Grove's quest for a state softball title and crush Joy's hopes for a scholarship to Iowa?

The thought chilled me.

Chapter
12

AT HOME IN THE APARTMENT ABOVE THE BAR, I SAT at my computer working on Mom's books for the tavern. I was keying the last of my entries into the computer when I heard Mom open and close the kitchen door.

"Jeremy?" she called.

"In my bedroom."

She came to the doorway, white-rimmed sunglasses riding on the top of her head. Mom was still slim and lithe in shorts and a sleeveless white T-shirt. I'd bet if she wanted to, she could still dance. It's probably not right for a guy to think of his mother as being sexy, or looking sexy. Maybe it's not so much that I thought she was sexy as it was the way I'd always see guys at the bar, even old guys, study her T-shirted bust line as she lifted her arms to draw a beer, or eye her butt as she turned and bent to reach in the bottom of the cooler. High on her left shoulder was tattooed a black rose. I remember once when I was twelve or thirteen running my fingertips across the rose, fascinated, and screwing up my courage to ask her why she'd gotten it.

"Young people often do very foolish things," she'd said, and smiled sadly. "Especially young girls. I worked in a place in Peoria called the Black Rose. The guy who owned it was named Tony Rose. I thought I was in love with him, the place, my job. . . ." She stroked my hair. "I was very foolish in those days, Jeremy." She smiled at me. "Promise me when you grow up you won't do foolish things."

"I won't, Mom. I promise."

Mom leaned against my bedroom door now. "Working on the books?"

I nodded. "You got any other bills or receipts lying around?"

"No." She took her sunglasses out of her hair. "I don't know what I'm going to do when you're gone, Jeremy."

"Same as before." I reached behind the computer and clicked it off. "Hire a bookkeeper."

"So easy for you to say."

"You'll find someone."

The telephone's ringing saved me from another

Why-did-you-join-the-navy? hassle with Mom. I took the call in the kitchen; it was Darin.

"What's up?" I asked.

"Just came back from therapy." He sounded pleased.

"Kind of tough to do therapy with a hangover, isn't it?"

"Don't sweat it. I'm doing great, improving all the time. Could be walking by the end of the year, driving a car."

"That's great, man."

He hesitated a moment. "About last night, old buddy. I'm sorry about last night."

"Sorry?"

"About getting on your case. You know, at my house. Calling you a jerk and all that."

"Forget it. You had too many beers. That was my fault. Hey, how come you didn't tell me your dad was going to AA?"

"Where did you hear that?"

"He told me last night. How come you didn't mention it?"

"He's got the problem. Not me. My problem is this chair. And everyone telling me what to do, when I can party, when I should go to bed—it's hell."

I pulled on the telephone cord and sat at the kitchen table.

Darin rambled on: "I keep thinking, Why me?

Am I being punished for something? What did I do? Then I think, Wait! I broke my neck, but my spinal cord was only traumatized. That's how the doctors say it. 'Traumatized.' I can come back. I'm going to be as good as new. You wait and see." Then he asked, "Did you see Joy today?"

"I caught the last half-hour of practice."

"How's she doing?"

"She was sick this morning. She didn't come back to your house last night and take you partying, did she?"

"I wish. The truth is I went straight to bed. Therapy, you know."

"I think she's coming down with a bad case of the flu."

"It's always something with her. What'd Thorton have to say to the girls?"

"The usual," I said. "He wants them to go out and kick ass. He's going to show them what it feels like to win it all."

"Jerk," Darin said. "He thinks he's so great. The thing is, if Joy shapes up, they *can* win it all. She's got to get the lead out, though, and keep her head in the game."

"She'll do OK. She's just got to shake this flu bug."

"What are you doing tonight?" Darin asked.

"Um . . . nothing. I haven't had much sleep lately.

I'll probably stay home, take it easy." I wasn't lying to him. That's exactly what I intended to do—after I helped Joy with her pitching.

"Joy say anything about doing something tonight?"

"I didn't ask her," I said. "She'll probably stay home, too. She's beat."

"Yeah. Well, that's what I wanted to know," Darin said. "I guess I'll stay home, as if I had a choice."

"Hey, it's not always going to be like that."

"You got that right," Darin said. "I read this story in a magazine the other day. It's about these stupid kids playing with a revolver. One kid shot another kid. The bullet blasted him in the face, went through his chin and lodged in his spine in the back of his neck. It bruised his spinal cord. Doctors couldn't take it out because it was too risky. So this kid went home a quad, and five years later he's normal. I mean, he walks and runs—except he's got this bullet in his neck. He was twelve when it happened. Hell, if some stupid little jerk like that can make it, I can, too. I don't even have a bullet in my neck. You wait and see. I'll play football again—"

I interrupted him. "Look, Darin, I've got to go."

"I will, I'll play football again."

"Sure you will."

"Call me tomorrow, OK?"

"Will do," I said, and hung up. Darin was in one of his up moods. I hoped he was right. I hoped he did come back and that he'd play football again, at least with buddies.

Chapter

13

I WAITED TILL NEARLY FIVE BEFORE I SKIPPED DOWN the Uptown's outside stairs in back of the building and stood in the sunshine. I cut between the tavern and the hardware store, crossed the street between parked cars, then sprinted through the town square. Huge maples dappled the grass with sunshine. I headed for the craft shop where Joy worked. She got off at five.

Inside, the craft store smelled of exotic woods and spices, scents that always made my nose twitch. I looked up and down the rows of wicker baskets, wooden figurines, and bolts of twine. I didn't see Joy. The owner, Mrs. Bradley, was at the register.

"Where's Joy? In the storeroom?" My nose twitched, and I sneezed. "Sorry."

Mrs. Bradley shook her head. "Sent her home."

"Sick?"

"She said she felt fine, but I remembered how done in she looked after the game yesterday, poor dear. She still looked peaked. 'You need your rest,' I told her. 'No need to be on your feet all afternoon. You take today and next week off. Make up your hours when Henry and me go on vacation,' I told her. So I sent her home."

"That was nice, Mrs. Bradley."

"We ain't so busy I can't handle the store a few days by myself. We need her to win that tournament."

"She will, Mrs. Bradley. She will. Don't worry." I headed for the door.

Newly painted white, Joy's house was an old two-story with lots of gables and a front porch running its width. A huge oak blocked the sun, shading the porch this time of day. When I pulled up and parked in front, Mrs. Kelley was sitting on a wooden swing hung from the ceiling, reading a book. The green swing matched the color of the shiny porch steps and floor.

She closed the book on her lap when I reached the top of the porch steps. "Jeremy, hi!"

Like Joy, she was lots of fun. You'd never guess she was a math teacher. She'd helped me so much with my math and computer skills, I'd never be able to repay her. The thing is, I'd taken only Algebra I and II from her. She'd taught me computer skills on her own time when I was a sophomore, letting me come into her classroom after school. By the time I took computer courses as a junior and senior, I was practically a whiz.

One time I told her, "I really appreciate this, Mrs. Kelley." I sat in front of a Macintosh in her classroom. I was finished for the afternoon and putting my disks away.

"You have a good mind for math and computers, Jeremy. You're willing to take time to learn. Kids like you are hard to find." She smiled at me. "Besides, except for Darin, you're Joy's best friend. Why wouldn't I help you?"

I felt my face turn red.

"What are your plans after you graduate?"

"I like electricity and electronics and math."

"There's a future for you in any of those areas, Jeremy."

"You think so?"

"I'm positive. Learn all you can. You'll see."

I remembered feeling great that afternoon because this woman had confidence in me simply because I was me. That's all, just me, Jeremy Logan. I wasn't a straight-A student, student body president, or an all-state jock. I was the kid of the widow who owned the tavern on Main Street.

"Joy home?" I asked now.

"In the house. Came home early from work. Said she felt all right, but I asked her to take a nap anyway. Surprise—she did."

"Maybe the pressure is getting to her," I said. "Everyone I talk to expects her to win the state tournament. They never talk about the rest of the team. They always ask about Joy, as if she's supposed to win the championship by herself."

"She tells me it's not the pressure. She's usually very good about sharing her problems with me, but she hasn't said what's bothering her—I've asked." Mrs. Kelley looked at me closely. "I thought perhaps she'd said something to you."

"I thought maybe she was getting a bad case of the flu. And she had that trouble on the mound yesterday because she forgot her Dramamine."

Mrs. Kelley looked surprised. "No. I made her take it before she left home."

I blinked. "Oh?"

"I always do. I know she won't remember it herself."

I didn't know what to say. I felt a stab of anger. Joy had lied to me. She had thrown up in a bucket all morning at practice and had let Coach Thorton think she had a hangover.

Another lie. Why?

An alarm went off in my mind and suddenly my brain was spinning.

Sick? In the morning?

I refused to believe what I was thinking. I locked the word out of my mind. I refused to let it touch my lips.

"Yeah, well, I just thought the way she looked yesterday, kind of pale, she forgot it."

"No," Mrs. Kelley said, "she took the pills."

Mrs. Kelley rocked back and forth in the swing, the chain squeaking where it was eye-hooked to the ceiling. "I don't mean to hurt your feelings, Jeremy, but there's something I should tell you."

"What?" I stuffed my hands into my jean pockets.

"I don't want you to misunderstand." Suddenly she sounded like Mr. Steele did last night, when he told me he didn't want me giving Jeremy anymore beer. I swallowed and prepared myself for the worst: she knew Joy and I were making love.

"I think after the tournament it's time this bond between you and Joy and Darin loosen a bit," she said.

"Loosen?"

"I don't mean that you three still shouldn't be friends, only that you should go your separate ways, now that you've graduated. You should let go of each other so all three of you can grow and develop. You and Joy are eighteen; Darin's nineteen—you're stifling one another."

I nodded. "Well, I'm going to the navy."

"A smart decision, Jeremy. Getting away will be good for you. Have you ever been to the East or West?"

I shook my head. "Just here. This is the only place I've been."

Mrs. Kelley looked at her hands. "Joy should select a school other than Iowa. She needs to be on her own and experience new people, away from you and Darin."

"I suppose you're right. What does Mr. Kelley say about her going to Iowa?"

"He won't hear of her going anywhere else. He graduated from there, you know. He wants to see her play, but he hopes in college she'll get interested in someone else besides Darin. We like Darin, but Joy has a life of her own. She should be dating lots of boys. Not just one."

"Um, what does Joy say about Iowa?"

"She's determined to go."

"Other good schools will offer her scholarships, even if Maple Grove doesn't win the state tournament."

"She knows that. I've told her, but she feels committed to Darin. Somehow he has a hold on her, a grip—"

"Mom!"

My head swung around. Joy stood in the doorway behind the screen door. "Hi," I said.

"Hi."

Joy swung the screen door open and stepped onto the porch, her hair tousled, her eyes puffy from sleep. The screen door banged closed.

"You've been listening to us?" her mother asked.

"Not on purpose. I woke up and heard voices. I came to the door." Joy looked me straight in the eye, shaking her head in rapid denial. "No one has a hold on me," she said, then looked at her mother. "I want you both to know that."

I nodded. "I'm sure your mother didn't mean it like it sounded. . . . I mean, like a stranglehold or something."

"Yes, I did." Mrs. Kelley stood up, the empty swing rocking back and forth. "Darin has a stranglehold on her. Joy and I have had this conversation before, haven't we?"

"Too many times."

Mrs. Kelley came to Joy and put the palm of her hand on Joy's forehead. "How do you feel, honey? You don't feel as if you've got a temperature."

"I'm all right. I needed some sleep."

"You want something to eat? Something light? Soup? A grilled cheese?"

"Nothing, Mom."

"I'll fix something anyway." Mrs. Kelley reached for the door.

"Mom, I don't want anything."

Mrs. Kelley forced a thin smile. "I know, but—"

"Nothing, Mom."

I piped up, "Actually, I wanted to take Joy over to school and go through her pitching motion. Maybe pitch a few to me."

"Do you feel up to it?" Mrs. Kelley asked Joy.

"I feel all right, I told you."

"It's better if Joy pitches from a mound, where she can face a plate and backstop. If she's hungry, we can get something on the way back."

Mrs. Kelley stood there with the screen door open, probably debating with herself whether or not she should protest. She smiled at us ruefully. "Well . . ."

Joy smiled back. "Flies are getting in, Mom."

"All right," Mrs. Kelley said. "What should I say if Darin calls again?"

"Tell him I'll see him later, about eight."

Chapter

14

"WHEN DID DARIN CALL?" I ASKED WHEN JOY CLIMBED into the Buick. I pulled away from the curb.

Though the Buick had sat in the shade of the oak tree, it was still hot inside. Joy had gone into the house for her glove and spikes. She wore gray cutoff sweatpants and a loose white T-shirt. She had brushed her hair back into a ponytail again.

"He called this afternoon," she said. "He wants me to come over tonight."

"What for?"

"He didn't say."

"I'll go with you."

"No . . . I have to go alone."

I glanced at her. "Why?"

She fidgeted with her glove, pulling at the laces.

"He . . . he said he wanted to see me alone, that's all."

The Buick had no air-conditioning. Hot air from the pavement blew in through the open windows. I headed toward the high school, only a mile away. I wasn't going to ask Joy about her Dramamine lie or mention the unspeakable fear in the back of my mind until after we worked out; otherwise, Joy would be too upset to concentrate. Or get so angry she'd go through the roof.

"You really feel better?" I asked.

"Just fine."

I parked in the faculty parking lot behind the school. Joy and I got out and walked across the grassy field toward the softball diamond, kicking up moths and bees from the dry grass and clover.

Her glove and spikes hanging from her right hand, Joy swung them back and forth as she walked along. I carried a catcher's glove and a new softball; I always stowed that kind of equipment in the trunk of my car, including a bat. Joy and I played catch in the park a lot. Or a game of slugger, if we could find enough people. Then I got a chance to bat against her. She could strike me out whenever she wanted to, but most of the time she let me hit the ball.

Fortunately, Maple Grove's old three-story brick school building was tall enough to block the sun this time of day, casting a shadow over the infield. Joy could work out in the shade.

I sat with her on the bleachers as she changed into her spikes. Kneading the new ball, catching its leathery smell, I told her, "Look, in your last five games—thirty-five innings—you've got fifty-two strikeouts but thirty-eight walks."

"I've won them all."

"I know. You should. Your ERA for that stretch is .47, but you're always in trouble. You nearly lost last night. Runners are always on base. Two great defensive plays saved you."

"I know."

"What I'm saying is, I know you want an Iowa scholarship, so you think you have to strike everybody out, but that's impossible. If you get the opportunity and need to strike somebody out, go for it. But if they want to swing at the first pitch and pop up or ground out, that's better for you. Pitch with finesse, conserve yourself, don't try to overpower everyone. You'll get into less trouble—fewer walks—and winning will be easier."

"Thorton always tells me I've got heat. 'Go get 'em,' he says. 'Mow 'em down, blow 'em away with your best!'"

"That's his football mentality."

"I have to do what he says."

"Joy, your best isn't fastball, fastball, fastball. It's

the fastball mixed with your other pitches: curve, drop, change-up."

She stood and held her hand out. "Give me the ball."

"Let's go through the motions first, OK?"

"Give me the ball."

"Just the motions. We want to check out your execution. Get out there on the mound." I slapped her on her butt, maybe a little too hard.

"Hey!" she yipped.

"Hay is for horses. Get out there." I crouched behind the plate, picked up some dust, and tossed it into the air. "Let's go."

Joy stood on the mound, right foot on the rubber, left foot eight inches behind it. She held the imaginary ball chest high in her glove. Then she leaned forward and rocked back; as she strode forward with her left foot, she began her windmill motion, releasing the imaginary ball as her left foot slammed the dirt two feet in front of the rubber.

"Looked good! Strike one!" I said.

"The next one will be so fast you won't even see it." She laughed.

"Try me."

She wound up and threw again.

"Ball one!" I yelled, and smiled.

"You're crazy!" Feigning anger, Joy threw her glove on the ground, dust leaping where it hit. "I protest!" She came off the mound, charging the plate. "You need glasses! You're blind."

I stood. "C'mon, Joy. Don't play around."

"I'm not playing around."

"You are, too." I pointed at the mound. "Get back there. Throw another twenty or thirty like that."

"Jeremy, this is the same stupid stuff I do in February, before the season starts."

"It won't hurt you." I snapped my fingers and pointed again. "Get!"

Joy threw twenty-five more imaginary pitches, her motion smooth, graceful, fluid—exactly the same every time, the way it should be. I was satisfied, so I tossed the ball to her. "Start out easy," I told her.

I crouched behind the plate and pounded the pocket of my glove. Without warning Joy fired a three-quarter-speed fastball at me. I threw my glove up—not to catch the damned ball—just to block it so it didn't bang off my forehead. "What the hell!" I cried, the ball rolling away. "What the hell are you trying to do?"

Joy spit on the ground like a major leaguer. "Be alert. That's for slapping my butt."

"Will you stop fooling around?" I said half-mad, and retrieved the ball by the backstop. "Get serious." I rubbed the ball and flipped it to her.

Standing on the mound, she gave a deep bow. "Yes, sir!"

She threw fifteen half-speed fastballs. Then slowly her pitches picked up velocity. I didn't tell her to increase the speed; she did it on her own. She began to sweat, the neck of her T-shirt wet. Soon her fastball sailed and danced, popping into my glove, always a strike, stinging my palm, shooting a streak of pain through my hand up to my elbow. She threw twenty stingers before I asked for mercy.

"Hey," I said. "How about the curve ball, the change-up? Let's work on 'em all." I reached in my back pocket for my handkerchief.

"What's wrong? Your hand hurt?" Joy grabbed the bottom of her T-shirt to wipe the sweat off her face.

"Don't worry about it," I said.

"What's the handkerchief for?"

"Just pitch." I folded the handkerchief and stuffed it inside the glove to cover my palm. "Let's see the curve."

We worked another twenty minutes. Joy's execution was perfect. Curve, drop, change-up—Joy's pitches spun, dove, floated. In a relaxed, fun, tension-free atmosphere, Joy Kelley could do practically anything she wanted with a softball. If she threw the proper assortment of pitches, no high school team in the state was going to belt her out of the game. Pressure, fatigue, nerves—those were her pitfalls.

And maybe something else.

When we decided to quit, I was sweaty, dusty, and thirsty. I wished I had a drink of cold water. Sweat soaked Joy's T-shirt, flattening it to her chest. I met her at the mound and felt heat radiating from her body. "You're looking good," I said.

"You really think so?" Puffing her cheeks, she blew out a long stream of air. "I feel OK."

"Your execution is perfect." I took her glove from her. "I think in the last couple of games, especially with the heat and humidity, you've been getting fatigued in the final innings. Or something else is wrong with you."

I fished my handkerchief out of my catcher's mitt and gave it to her so she could wipe the sweat off her face.

She gave me a sidelong glance. "What's that mean?" She wiped her face and neck.

I couldn't say the word.

"You didn't forget to take your Dramamine yesterday. Your mother made sure you took it. She told me."

Joy looked at me sharply. "So, now you're checking up on me, Jeremy? Is that it?"

"You threw up all morning at practice. You lied to Coach Thorton, letting him think you had a hangover."

"That's my business."

I still couldn't say the word.

"You were sick all *morning*, Joy. I'm slow, but I'm not stupid."

"Leave me alone." She threw my handkerchief at me and started marching toward the car.

"When's the last time you had your period?"

She halted, whirled, and shot me a piercing look. "Jeremy! That's none of your business."

"It *is* my business. And the answer might explain why you're having such a tough time on the mound lately."

"You're crazy."

"Look!" I said. "We hit it lucky the first time."

"And you've used a condom ever since."

"But one of them came off. Remember?"

"Jeremy, I don't want to talk about this."

"Are you pregnant?"

The dreaded word was finally out, and it numbed my lips.

"No!"

"Joy, this has got me scared. Really scared."

"How do you think I feel?" she asked.

"If you're pregnant, I can't imagine. . . ." I took a breath. "You know what it says on condom packages? No contraceptive provides one hundred percent protection from pregnancy. It says a condom can only *aid* in the prevention of pregnancy. That's all! There are no guarantees."

"I can't be pregnant."

"Denial won't change anything."

"I can't be!"

"Joy, I'm going to tell you something again. I know you don't want me to say it—"

"Jeremy, whatever you're going to say—"

"—but I've got to say it anyway."

"Jeremy, please—"

"I love you, Joy. I have from day one." I circled her in my arms and held her tightly, feeling her wet T-shirt on my chest.

"Jeremy, please don't say you love me."

I stepped back and held her by the shoulders. Tears pooled in her eyes.

"Is this why you've been lying lately? Why you said we had to stop? You're afraid you're pregnant?"

She nodded. "But I don't want to know anything till after the tournament."

"You've suspected all along, haven't you?"

"Maybe Coach Thorton or my parents won't let me pitch. The whole damned town will find out why, and I will have let everyone down. Everyone's counting on me."

"Women run marathons when they're two, three, four months pregnant, don't they? I'll bet nobody will say you can't pitch. Besides, if you are, you can't be that far along."

"Oh, Jeremy . . ."

A terrible sinking, hollow feeling invaded my stomach. I felt as if *I* had to throw up. What had I done? What should I do? Maybe there was no reason to panic. Maybe the stress of softball and of dealing with Darin and me had caused Joy to miss her period. The first thing we had to do was find out if Joy was really pregnant or not.

I said, "Listen, we have to find out the truth so we can figure out what to do. If we know, maybe we can get you something for morning sickness. Maybe we can work on a pitching strategy so you could save energy. I don't know. . . . Besides, Coach Thorton says if you throw up at practice again, he's going to call your parents. There must be some kind of over-the-counter pills you can get for morning sickness. But maybe you've just got some stupid virus."

"Could be," Joy said.

"If we find out you're not pregnant, that'll take a lot of pressure off. Then you can go to a doctor and get a prescription—penicillin or something—to knock out the virus. *Wham!* You're ready to win a state title. The key is, we've got to find out."

"All right."

I kissed her, tasting the sweat beads above her upper lip. "I love you. Get in the car."

Chapter
15

Fifteen minutes later, I parked the Buick in front of a Walgreen drugstore in Riverbend.

"I can't believe you're going to do this," Joy said.

"We've got to know the truth so we can deal with it."

"Who's going in?"

"I will," I said. "Everyone knows who you are."

I'd bought only one package of condoms in my life, a twenty-four pack, but I didn't buy it in Maple Grove. I knew everyone who worked at the drugstore, and Mom didn't have vending machines in the rest rooms at the tavern. So I bought the twenty-four pack at this Walgreen store in Riverbend.

The last time I was here, searching the store for condoms, hoping I didn't have to ask the druggist or a clerk, I found them in an aisle labeled Health Care.

I went to the same aisle. Strategically placed next to the condoms was what I was looking for: pregnancy-testing kits. What a clever piece of marketing: buy condoms for safe sex, but don't forget to pick up a pregnancy-testing kit for later. Three or four kinds of kits stared at me. One kind was probably as good as the other. I grabbed one and hurried toward the register, thankful there was no line.

The woman at the check-out counter was the same one who had checked me out when I bought the condoms. She was about fifty, wearing half-glasses, the kind older people wear halfway down their noses. She smiled. *Did she remember me?*

"Is that all, young man?"

I reached for my wallet. "Yes."

She picked up the kit, turned it over and over, looking for its price. She peered at me over the top of her glasses with watery blue eyes. "This isn't marked. Do you remember the price?"

I cleared my throat. "I, uh, just grabbed it."

"There are several different testing kits. Some are easier to use than others. Is this the one you want?"

"Um . . . this one will be OK."

A middle-aged man with a mustache and a girl, thirteen or fourteen, stepped in line behind me. The man carried a twelve-pack of beer and the girl clutched several magazines rolled up in her hands.

I shifted from one foot to the other.

"I'll have to check the price." The clerk set the kit on the counter. "Be right back. Good evening, Charlie . . . Melody," she said.

"Evening, Vera," the man said.

"Hello, Mrs. Holmes," the girl said. She tilted her head and looked at my purchase on the counter. Then she smiled at me and said, "Hi."

The man frowned and nudged her in the back. He probably didn't want his daughter talking to a guy buying a pregnancy-testing kit, but her smile grew wider. "Aren't you Jeremy Logan?"

"Yes . . . yes, I am."

"I'm Melody Albright, pitcher for the eighth grade. We live on a farm just south of here."

Now I recognized her. She was a Maple Grove Junior High pitcher. Some said she'd be as good as Joy by the time she was a senior.

"Oh, hi," I said. "How you doing?"

"Just great. Are we going to win? Is Joy OK?"

"We're going to win. Joy's great."

"I was just wondering," the girl said. "I saw the last game; she looked beat."

"Joy's just fine," I assured her.

"Are you her boyfriend? I see you with her lots."

"Uh, no . . . as a matter of fact I'm not. She, uh . . . goes with someone else."

The clerk hustled back behind the counter, saying, "Sorry I took so long."

"That's all right."

She rang up the price on the register, and I laid out some bills next to the kit. "You want that in a bag?" she asked.

"Yes, please."

"Have you read the directions?" She looked at me over the top of her glasses again.

"Directions?"

"For the kit," she said. "You've got to follow the directions for all these pregnancy-testing kits carefully. Have you read them?"

"No . . . no, I haven't. It's not for me." I smiled.

Only Melody smiled with me.

"It's got to be used first thing in the morning," the clerk said, "else you've wasted your money." She handed me my change.

"All right."

"I hope Joy's OK," Melody said. "Tell her good luck."

"I will," I said, and spun on my heels.

"Remember, first thing in the morning," the woman called to my back as I hit the door.

Outside I let out a deep breath. The hot sun reflecting off the sidewalk and parked cars was so bright I had to squint. The temperature was probably eighty, but I felt a lot cooler outside than I had inside, in the air-conditioned drugstore.

When I climbed into the Buick, Joy looked as if she'd been roasting. I handed her the brown paper bag.

She looked inside and said, "I can't believe you actually bought this."

"It was no big deal. Take it home and find out the truth." I smiled. "If you don't use it, I want my money back. OK?"

She looked into the bag again, then nodded. "A-OK," she said.

Joy and I didn't talk on the way home: each of us had too much to think about. My number-one priority was her condition, her health. Winning the tourney was second. Explaining things to Darin, Joy's parents, and my mom—that came last.

Butterflies fluttered into my stomach. I was scared. That's the only word I could think of. *Scared*. Like me, she had to be totally, absolutely, honestly *scared*.

Three months ago she was dancing and laughing with her buddies at the Junior-Senior Prom . . . making love later. Now she was maybe pregnant, stricken with morning sickness, and faced with the task of pitching Maple Grove to the state softball title.

Suddenly flashes of ugly scenes between Mr. and

Mrs. Kelley and me, my mom and me, Thorton and me, and Darin and me flashed through my mind.

I didn't know anything about babies. I'd never held a baby. What would Joy and I do with a baby? What about her softball career? What about college? Had I ruined her life?

I felt sick.

We pulled up in front of Joy's house at seven-thirty, the sun a red ball just starting to sink behind her house. The air was hot and still; wilted leaves hung lifelessly in the trees.

"What have you been thinking about?" I asked.

"About Darin. What I'm going to tell him if I am pregnant. How am I going to tell my mom and dad? They've always trusted me. What about college? What will I do with a baby?" Her expression was bleak. "What have you been thinking about?"

"The same stuff, but mostly about you. I want you to be all right."

"I'll be OK." Joy gathered her spikes and glove from the floor of the car. "I have to go in, Jeremy."

"People have a sixth sense when it comes to us," I said.

"What do you mean?"

"My mother suspects I like you. A girl I just saw in the drugstore asked if you were my girlfriend."

"Who?"

"Melody Albright."

"Oh, no. Did she see what you bought?"

"I told her you went with someone else. She doesn't know the kit's for you. And Hazel said to me the other morning, 'See your girlfriend won.' " I shrugged and scratched my head. "People just seem to know. You're probably right: Darin knows, too."

Joy didn't answer.

"Well . . . maybe there's some other reason you missed your period, and this problem isn't as bad as it seems."

"I hope you're right."

"Call tomorrow. Promise?"

"Promise," she said.

Chapter
16

DURING THE SUMMER, DELIVERING A MORNING PAPER route was great. The mornings were cool and dewy, stars and streetlights lighting the way. Near the end of the route, about 5:30 A.M., I'd see the sky turning scarlet in the east, a pale light replacing darkness, while sparrows, robins, and cardinals began their morning chatter. My route covered ten miles and included not only Maple Grove but also Darin's subdivision of Sunnyside. Letting the car idle, I ran from house to house, delivering the paper to the precise spot required: mailbox, screen door, side door. Then I'd pop back into the car and drive to the next cluster of houses.

When I delivered the next morning, I couldn't stop my mind from racing forward and asking more questions about the future. *If Joy was pregnant, would she have the baby or an abortion? Joy in college, me in the navy—how could we be together? How could Joy take a baby to college with her, study, and play softball? Would her parents want to raise another child? Would my mom raise a baby?*

Wait!

A baby would be Joy's and my responsibility. Not our parents'. But I'd be away in the navy.

After I finished my route, I often stopped at the Mac Shack, ordered breakfast, and ate it at the Uptown. That morning I sat at the center of the bar in the Uptown, under the Old Style sign that hung from the ceiling. I ate my two Egg McMuffins, sipped a bottle of pop, and read the sports pages.

The state softball tournament took top billing right below the fold, a byline story:

IHSAA ANNOUNCES STATE PAIRINGS

By Jim Kelley, Sports Editor

The Iowa High School Athletic Association announced today the pairings for the 16-team field competing for the girls' state softball championship to be held in Riverbend, beginning Monday. . . .

I finished eating. I thought about hiding Hazel's paper in a cooler but decided against it. I went as quietly as I could up the creaky stairs. I didn't want to wake Mom; she loved to sleep late.

I couldn't sleep that morning. I was too nervous, too rattled. I decided to try to read while I waited for Joy's call. I was into self-improvement books lately but hadn't had much time to read. In fact, I'd started this one a month ago and had waded to only page seventy-six. Titled *Seeds of Success*, the book was supposed to reveal the ten best-kept secrets of total success. I'd bought it in paperback at the used bookstore.

I couldn't read, either. I couldn't concentrate on the words. When the phone rang, a chill shot through me. This phone call could affect the rest of my life. I leapt out of the chair, my book tumbling to the floor, and caught the phone in the kitchen in the middle of the third ring. My heart pounded against my breastbone. "Hello?"

"What's up. Why are you out of breath?" It was Darin . . . only *Darin!*

"What do you want?" I slumped into a chair at the table.

"You want to go to Joy's practice this morning?"

I rubbed my eyes and thought a moment. "Yeah, sure. I'll go. What time you want me to pick you up?"

"Practice starts at nine. How about eight-thirty?"

"Fine. No therapy today?"

"This afternoon."

"What'd you do last night?"

"Joy came over."

"Oh, yeah?" I yawned again, this time into the phone, trying to fake disinterest. "What'd you do?"

"We had a special time, man."

"Special?" I said. The word *special* wasn't one Darin used to describe an evening. "A blast," "a ball," "a kinky good time"—those were expressions typical of Darin.

"We went out," he said. "Rode around and parked. I'm a man again, Jeremy."

His words jolted me, and I sat up straight. "What's that mean?"

"What do you think it means?"

"It means you and Joy—?"

He laughed. "Not yet. I'm working on it. I'm a man, I know that." He paused, as if he were waiting for my congratulations, but I was silent. "See you at eight-thirty," he said. "I need to talk to you."

"Right. Eight-thirty."

Talk about what?

I hung up and dropped my head back, staring at the ceiling. Darin was a man again. That meant Joy's kissing him—their making out—was rejuvenating him. It was sex therapy.

The phone rang again, startling me a second time. I jerked the receiver to my ear. "Hello?"

"Hi, it's me." Joy sounded subdued. "What were you doing, sitting on the phone?"

"You could say that. How are you feeling?"

"Not so good, but I'll be all right."

"You've got to get a prescription or something. Seeing a doctor would be your best bet."

She didn't answer.

"Did you take the test?"

She sighed deeply. "Yes."

"Well . . . ?"

"I'm pregnant. . . ."

My heart lurched.

"We can't see each other anymore."

"How can we not see each other?" I said. "How can we avoid it?"

"It's over, Jeremy. I don't even want to talk to you."

"We've got decisions to make," I said.

"I'll handle them."

"Not without me you can't."

"It's my problem."

"*Ours*, Joy. It's *our* problem."

"I have to go now."

"Joy, I love you!"

"I never said I loved *you!*"

"You don't love Darin—"

I heard a sharp click, then the dial tone. I stared at the phone. Cursing, I slammed the receiver into place.

"What was that all about?"

I looked up to see Mom in the doorway, wrapped in her old pink robe, curly hair tangled. When she wasn't wearing makeup, I could tell she was getting older. Wrinkles lined the corners of her eyes and mouth. She'd spent too many nights in smoke-filled bars, though she didn't smoke or drink anymore. She told me a month ago, "I gave up drinking and smoking long ago so I'd live long enough to watch you grow up. Now you're going to the navy."

"Something wrong?" she asked now.

"Nothing." My face felt like fire.

"Nothing? I heard the phone ring twice this morning. I heard you yelling at Joy."

"How did you know I was talking to Joy?"

She looked at me and smiled. "I heard you say her name." Mom stepped into the kitchen. "I heard you say, 'I love you, Joy.'"

I shook my head. "That doesn't mean a thing."

"What's going on, Jeremy?"

"Nothing!" I got up and shoved my chair back to the table. "You have no right to listen to my telephone conversations."

"I wasn't listening purposely. I could have heard your voice anywhere in the house."

"I'm eighteen. I can't do anything around here without your checking on me. That's why I'm joining the navy." I stomped into my bedroom and slammed the door. As soon as I fell on the bed, I was sorry I'd yelled at Mom. I'd had a chance right there to tell her about Joy and me, about the mess we were in, but I was too chicken.

Chapter

17

MRS. STEELE AND DARIN WERE WAITING FOR ME on their front porch at eight-thirty. The morning sky was clear blue, temperature in the seventies, headed for ninety-five at noonday. Mrs. Steele was dressed in a red bikini. From my car, I took her in with a sweep of my eyes, then got out and waved "Hi" to them. I walked up Darin's ramp.

"I want him home by twelve," Mrs. Steele said. "He has to be in therapy by one."

"No problem." I stepped around Darin's chair and tilted it back, catching a whiff of Mrs. Steele's perfume.

"What *am* I?" Darin piped up. "You talk about me like I'm luggage." His long, glossy black hair was pulled back and held with a rubberband, a diamond earring stuck in his left earlobe.

"Darin, I'm sure your mother didn't mean anything."

"I'll be home when I want to!"

"Sweetheart . . . ," Mrs. Steele said.

"See you," I said to Mrs. Steele, and wheeled Darin down the ramp to his van. I loaded him in with the lift and secured his chair. He was silent as I drove away from his house. What did he want to talk to me about? I hoped he wasn't working himself into one of his down moods, though he'd sounded up earlier on the phone.

"The progress you're making in therapy is really great," I said, breaking the silence. "Do the doctors say you'll walk again?"

"They never tell you stuff like that. They don't want to look bad, in case they're wrong. But I will." Then he said, "Guess what?"

"What?" Darin had already shaken me with his announcement about being a man. I didn't know if I could stand another shock.

"I gave Joy a ring last night," he said.

I was in the midst of stopping for the intersection leading out of Sunnyside to the highway. I was going maybe five miles an hour, but I hit the brakes so hard and stopped so sharply, I nearly hurled Darin and myself through the van's windshield.

"What's wrong with you?" he yelled. "All I need is whiplash."

"Sorry," I said, trying to get my thoughts together.

"You going to stop here all day?"

I pulled onto the highway. I waited for him to tell me what kind of ring. My mind reeled. Was it an engagement ring? Joy wouldn't accept an engagement ring. She couldn't. She was going to have *our* baby. I couldn't wait any longer. "What kind of ring?" I said.

"Pre-engagement," he said.

"Oh . . ."

"Got a problem with that?"

"Why should I?"

"You don't sound so happy. Sometimes I think you spend more time with Joy than I do."

"I spend time with both of you. So you're engaged to be engaged, is that it?"

"Sort of. She doesn't want to become engaged officially. She says there are too many uncertainties in her life. I told her to win this tournament and get an Iowa scholarship. I'd do my part and walk again. That would take care of the uncertainties."

"What'd she say?"

"She said she'd do her best." He paused a second. "Are you making it with her?"

The question was a shot from a cannon fired point-blank at my back, hitting me between the shoulder blades. I should've been ready for the shot: Joy had warned me Darin suspected; I sensed as much myself, but I wasn't close to being ready. I tensed. My heart revved and the tips of my ears burned. I thought of guys taking lie detector tests. How fast did their hearts beat when they knew they were going to lie? The thing is, I wanted to tell him the truth: *We're making love, Darin. Joy's pregnant.* He was going to find out soon anyway, but Darin's knowing the truth now—at this moment—would upset Joy so much she'd never throw a strike in the tournament. She'd walk the Leafs straight to defeat.

I had no choice. I had to lie.

I steeled myself. "No," I said, "I'm not making it with her."

"What took you so long to answer? Thinking of a lie?"

"If I was making it with her, I'd have a lie ready."

"Like what?"

"I don't know. I'm not making it with her. Is that why you've been such a creep lately? You think Joy and I are doing it?"

"This is about *you*—not me."

"We're not," I said.

We stopped the night before last.

"You always stick up for her," Darin said. "I've seen how you look at each other. You take her home every night. There's nothing going on?"

"Nothing."

"I practically had to force her to take my ring. Why is that? Are you the reason?"

"She's not ready for that kind of commitment," I said. "She has college and a softball career ahead of her."

Darin was silent. I wanted to glance at him in the rearview mirror to see if I could read his face, his eyes, to see if he believed me, but I didn't dare look: I feared my own face, my own eyes would betray me.

"I thought I could trust both of you," Darin said.

My fingers worked on the steering wheel. "You can."

"You're not the skinny nerd you used to be."

"Thanks. I'll take that as a compliment."

When Darin let the matter drop, I was relieved, yet I felt terrible. I'd never been a liar. I hated being one now. My solution to this complicated mess was becoming clear. As soon as the state tourney was over, no matter what the price, no matter how scared we were, Joy and I would have to be honest with everyone. We'd have to tell Darin, his parents, Joy's parents, and my mom what had happened and go from there. The thought numbed me.

Chapter
18

I PARKED IN THE LOT BEHIND SCHOOL, LOWERED DARIN out of the van, and started pushing him in his wheelchair across the field to the girls' softball diamond. The sun was beginning to feel warm. I hadn't gone twenty yards when I spotted Joy sitting alone in the dugout with her head down.

Though practice didn't start till nine, most of the girls were in the outfield tossing balls back and forth.

"What's Joy doing in the dugout?" Darin asked.

"I don't know."

"She's just sitting there."

I knew practice was going to be late starting because Mr. Kelley was standing behind the backstop talking to Coach Thorton, notebook and pencil in hand, getting a story. I wheeled Darin around them and stopped behind the third-base dugout, where Joy was still sitting alone.

"What's up?" I peered through the dugout's wooden slats.

She turned around, surprised to hear my voice. "What are you doing here?"

"Darin wanted to stop."

Grabbing her glove and getting up slowly, she came out of the dugout to where Darin and I waited. She looked peaked again.

"Why were you just sitting there?" Darin said.

She's got morning sickness. Leave her alone.

"You kept me out too late." Joy forced a smile and kissed Darin.

I winced.

"You should know better than to stay out late," I told her.

"Just slow getting started, that's all."

"Where's your ring?" Darin said.

"In the car. We can't wear jewelry during practices and games. You know that."

Suddenly the shrill sound of Thorton's whistle cut the air. "All right, ladies!" he cried. "Get the lead out!"

The players dropped what they were doing and circled up in center field, sitting in the grass. Thorton roamed the circle, lecturing, shaking his finger at them. He was too far away for us to hear what he was saying.

I pushed Darin over to the bleachers behind the backstop and sat next to him two rows up. Mr. Kelley came over, climbed up behind me and sat, still scribbling on his notepad. Parents drifted across the vacant field toward the bleachers with the players' younger brothers and sisters in tow.

"What's Thorton say about our chances?" Darin asked Mr. Kelley.

Mr. Kelley didn't answer. He was still scribbling frantically on his notepad. Finally he punctuated his last entry with an exclamation point. "What?" he said.

"Are we going to win?" Darin asked.

"It's going to be tough." He stuck his pen in his shirt pocket. "There are some good teams from the northwestern part of the state. And you know Riverbend is tough. Then there's always a sleeper— some little school, a hundred kids in high school, thirty girls—some sleeper that rises up, surprises the hell out of everyone, and knocks off the big guys. You can never take anybody or anything for granted, but we can win if things work out."

"If Joy gets on the stick?" Darin asked. "Is that what you mean?"

"She's not the whole team," I said.

"Thorton says he's going to pitch her every game. I told him go ahead. Work is what she needs."

"We have to win four straight games to win the tournament," I said. "If Thorton pitches her all twenty-eight innings, he's crazy. In this heat he'll burn her out."

"She's not fragile," Darin said.

"She's a Kelley," Mr. Kelley said. "She'll mow 'em down. I don't call her 'Killer' for nothing."

"Right." I nodded.

Thorton finished his lecture in center field. The team did stretches for five minutes, then ran wind sprints from left field to right field. After that, the infielders came in to play their positions and work on fielding bunts with runners on. The outfielders did the bunting and ran the bases.

Joy pitched for the workout. I could tell she was hurting. Every pitch, every move to field the ball, every throw to a base was misery for her. She was executing listlessly and not attacking the ball.

I knew exactly what she was doing. She was telling herself she wasn't sick; she was burying "sick" in her mind and practicing no matter how she felt. Her mind was telling her body, *Do it!* but her body was saying, *Give me a break!* Just watching her hurt me.

After she threw the ball into the dirt twice—once to first, the other time to second—Thorton yelled at her: "Kelley, out of there! Meyer, take over!"

Joy didn't argue; she trudged off the mound, pounding the pocket of her glove, head hanging.

"She looks bad," Darin said.

"Something's definitely wrong with her," Mr. Kelley said.

Annie Meyer took over on the mound. "What's Thorton say about Meyer's shoulder?" I asked Mr. Kelley.

"She's ready to go, coach."

"She's no pitcher," Darin said. "And Joy doesn't look good. I'd say we're in trouble."

Contrary to what Darin thought, Annie Meyer was a good pitcher. A left-handed sophomore, five-eight, a hundred-fifty pounds, she was a big, muscular farm girl with a smile for everyone. Her fastball tailed away from left-handed hitters, and her curve broke sharply in on the hands of right-handed hitters. But that's all she had: fastball, curve. Most good pitchers have three or four pitches. Despite her limited assortment of pitches, Annie was 2–1 for the season with a 1.50 ERA. After Annie, Thorton didn't have much left, a junior and a senior who hadn't thrown in a game all year.

Out of the corner of my eye, while Thorton was on the mound talking to Annie, I saw Joy slipping out of the dugout. She walked quickly down the left-field line toward the parking lot. God, was she walking out of practice? Thorton was hard-nosed. He'd bench her for that. He'd take a loss rather than play a star who defied him. At least that's the way he coached football. Neither Darin nor Mr. Kelley noticed Joy's leaving. I waited till she was lost among the cars in the lot, and then I stood up.

"I'll be right back, Darin."

Mr. Kelley was studying his notes.

"Where you going?"

"Don't worry about it," I said.

I stepped out of the stands and raced by the dugout, then down the third-base line. Thorton was screaming at the infielders: "Keep your eye on the ball when you field it—not the runner!" I had to stop Joy before she got into her car and drove away.

I found her by the car, all right, but she wasn't getting in and driving away. She was standing by the driver's door, feet apart, bent over, hands on her hips, sounding as if she had the dry heaves.

When she heard me approach, she straightened and glared at me, her eyes glassy from the strain of throwing up.

"Leave me alone, Jeremy!" She wiped the corners of her eyes with her fingertips, and I gave her my handkerchief. She grabbed it and wiped her mouth. "Thanks. Now leave me alone."

"I thought maybe you were walking out of practice."

"No way. I just needed someplace where I could be alone."

"You need to see a doctor."

"I'll handle it."

"And we need to have a long talk about what we're going to do."

She bent and looked at her face in the car's side mirror. She smoothed back her hair and wiped her mouth again with my handkerchief. "I have to get back to practice."

"Talk to me, Joy! Talk to me!" I was mad now—tired of being ignored. I slammed the roof of her car with the flat of my hand—her mother's car, actually, a red Escort. "Talk to me! Did Darin give you a ring?"

"It's a friendship ring!"

"That's not what he thinks. He thinks you and he are practically engaged."

"That's not true."

"Don't lie, Joy. Don't do that again. Talk to me. I want to know what's going on."

"Nothing!"

"*Nothing?* We're going to have a baby, and you practically get yourself engaged to another guy, and you won't even talk to me! That's nothing?"

She wiped sweat off her forehead with her palm.

"What's going on?"

"Leave it alone, Jeremy. We'll all be better off."

I swallowed, almost afraid to say what had popped into my mind. "You're thinking abortion, aren't you?"

Suddenly we both saw Mr. Kelley walking across

the field toward us. "My father's coming." Joy bent and gave herself a last look in the Escort's mirror. "I have to go."

I grabbed her wrist. "Meet me after work."

"I'm not going to work."

I'd forgotten Mrs. Bradley had given Joy time off. Joy tried to yank her wrist free, but I wouldn't let go. "Then meet me this afternoon. Or I'm going to keep us right here till your old man spots us. He'll want to know what's going on. I'll tell him everything."

She gave her wrist another jerk, but I held on. Mr. Kelley was nearly at the blacktop. I don't know if he'd seen us or not. Joy looked desperate.

"Two-thirty. The cemetery." I squeezed her wrist harder.

She shook her head, and tried to pry my fingers away.

"When?" I demanded, barely able to hold my grip on her.

Her eyes blazed. "Four!" She threw my hand-kerchief at me.

"All right. Four."

"I'll meet you"—her face was fire now—"but it'll be the *last* time we see each other!"

Chapter
19

I COULD HAVE WALKED AROUND THE SCHOOL BUILDING, then back to the softball diamond along the right-field line, avoiding Mr. Kelley, but I wasn't in the mood to go out of my way for anybody. I swung away from Joy and stomped across the parking lot. How could Joy tell me our next meeting would be our last? Abortion, that was how. The baby was living in her body, not mine. She had exclusive rights to the baby. She didn't have to ask me about an abortion.

Mr. Kelley and I halted in front of each other on the edge of the blacktop. "What's going on, coach?" he asked. "I look up and you're gone. Joy's gone. Darin says you ran to the parking lot. What's going on?"

I was in no mood to make excuses, either, yet I couldn't tell him the truth. Not yet. Not now. Another lie: "Nothing."

Mr. Kelley eyed me. "You look upset. Darin's upset. He said you and Joy weren't to be trusted. What's that mean? Is something wrong between the three of you?"

"Nothing's wrong."

"You sure? Darin's fit to be tied."

"Everything's fine." I brushed by Mr. Kelley and headed for the bleachers.

When I looked up, I saw Darin pushing himself across the field in his wheelchair, headed toward me.

I threw up my hands and yelled, "Hey, not so fast! Where do you think you're going?"

Mouth open, he was sweating and breathing hard. He'd come about forty yards, the farthest I'd ever seen him push himself. "What's going on? Where's Joy?" His head jerked.

"She's in the parking lot by her car."

"Why?" he demanded.

"I don't know. She made those two bad throws. I thought maybe she hurt herself."

"Did she?"

"No. She . . . went to get an aspirin. She said she's got a headache."

Darin's eyes narrowed suspiciously. "What are you guys hiding?"

"Nothing."

Finished talking to her father, Joy came trotting toward us. "What's going on?" Darin asked when she halted in front of him.

"I told you," I cut in and looked quickly at Joy.

"Let her answer!" Darin said.

"She went to get an aspirin," I added.

Joy nodded. "That's right. My shoulder hurts. I got an aspirin."

"Shoulder?" Darin asked.

Joy didn't know what to say next. She looked at me for help.

I said, "You better get back before Thorton has a cow."

"Yeah, right. See you later."

I watched her trot back along the left-field line. Spotting her, Thorton called her over, talked to her, then pointed at the dugout. She walked slowly away.

"You said she had a headache," Darin said.

"I *thought* she had a headache."

"Somebody's lying. She said her shoulder hurts."

"So her shoulder hurts," I said. "I don't know what's wrong with her."

From where Darin and I stood, we watched the team work on the cutoff play, the outfielders throwing the ball into the pitcher, who tried to cut advancing base runners down with a perfect peg to one of the bases. Joy took her turn on the mound last, executing perfectly, thank God, nailing two runners. I was happy for that, but I decided I didn't want to stay till the end of practice. I didn't want Darin to get Joy and me together and ask us point-blank if we were having sex, as he'd asked me earlier. Joy and I hadn't rehearsed. I didn't think we could improvise and lie convincingly enough to fool him.

I tilted Darin's chair back. "Let's go."

"Wait!" he yelled. "Practice isn't over. I want to talk to Joy."

"Call her up."

Darin swung his head around and tried to look at me. His face was red, and he was so mad I thought he was going to jump out of his chair. "You jerk!" he said. "I want to stay!"

"I didn't say I was going to stay all morning. You wanted to watch practice, so I came over for a while. Now we're leaving."

"You are getting to be a *real* jerk, Jeremy." I pushed Darin across the grass toward the parking lot. The sun was a lot warmer now. I could feel myself sweating.

I expected Darin to yell all the way home about our leaving early, but he didn't. He fell into his silent mood. I was almost certain he didn't believe the lie I'd told him in the van this morning, but I didn't think he could possibly guess Joy was pregnant.

After I wheeled the van into Darin's drive and stopped, we both sat silently a moment. "Well, I got you home in plenty of time for therapy," I said. "Your mom will be happy about that." I turned in the captain's chair to smile at him.

Darin's stare was ice. "Why didn't you want me to talk to Joy?"

"Why would I care if you talk to Joy?"

"You lied to me this morning."

"You're paranoid, man. You need a shrink."

"You lied!"

"There's nothing to lie about. Joy accepted your ring, didn't she?"

"She didn't want to."

"But she did, so shut up."

Avoiding Darin's look, I lowered him out of the van to the drive. As I rolled him up the ramp, Mrs. Steele came to the door. Her body gleaming with suntan lotion, she had changed into a yellow bikini that was patches held together with strings. She'd slipped into her terry-cloth robe, open in front.

Don't look, Jeremy.

"Back so soon?" She held the screen door open for us, and I pushed Darin into the chilly, air-conditioned house.

"Yeah, well . . . I had to cut it short," I said. "Things to do."

I glanced at Darin. I wished I hadn't. His dark eyes were hard on me, deep into me. "Going back to pick up Joy?"

"No," I said.

Mrs. Steele's eyes darted from Darin to me; she sensed the tension. "Aren't both of you thirsty from being in the sun all morning?" she said. "Wouldn't you like a glass of lemonade, a Pepsi?"

I said, "Nothing for me, thank you."

"Except Joy."

"Darin! Stop that!" Mrs. Steele said.

"I can't walk," he said, "but I can *see!* He tries to be with her whenever he can—always behind my back. That's why you took me home early. Admit it!"

"I'd better go," I said.

"Right," Darin snorted. "Run to her."

My face hot, I whirled for the door. Mrs. Steele was right behind me.

"Jerk!" Darin was yelling at me as his mother closed the front door behind her. We stood on the porch in the brilliant sunlight.

"Don't leave him in there alone," I said. "He won't like our talking behind his back."

Looking at me solemnly, Mrs. Steele touched my shoulder with a warm hand, her rings gleaming in the sun. "Jeremy, tell me there's nothing between you and Joy. Tell me there isn't, so I can tell him I heard you say it. We all trust you. We all want Darin to be happy, don't we?"

"Yes."

"Tell me. . . ."

I swallowed. "There's nothing between us, Mrs. Steele. Nothing." I'd told so many lies today I couldn't count them. I took her hand from my shoulder. "I have to go."

She stroked my cheek. Her suntan lotion smelled like coconut. "Jeremy, I told you I'm here for you. You don't have to chase Joy. I'm here every day." She kissed me on the lips, and a shiver shot up my spine. "Come see me, please?"

"I—I have to go," I sputtered. "I have to go. I really have to go."

"Jeremy, don't be afraid."

I did an about-face. On rubbery legs, I raced to my car, fell in, and drove away like a madman.

Chapter
20

No one ever told me about sex. I mean, I took health class in high school and studied the unit about sex titled Human Relationships. I learned all the body parts and their functions; I studied their pictures in the text. I learned about the dangers of sex: pregnancy, venereal disease, AIDS. I'd watched R-rated movies on HBO and had seen pictures in books. I knew how to do it. And I was eighteen, a high school graduate, ready to handle whatever the adult world had to throw at me.

Wrong!

Pain, frustration, confusion, desperation—no one ever mentioned those words in the sex unit I'd studied in high school or in the R-rated movies I'd watched. No one ever said, "The emotional turmoil will rip your guts out." I guess there was some emotional turmoil in the movies I'd seen, but the movies always ended happily. I couldn't foresee a happy ending to the situation Darin, Joy, and I were in. No way. If someone would have mentioned "emotional turmoil," I wouldn't have believed them anyway. Nothing could have prepared me for what was happening now. Sex had turned my life into a maze. Where was the fun?

When I got home from Darin's that morning, Mom was gone. I took the *Playboy* calendar off the back of my closet door and sat on my bed, leafing through April, May, June, July. I didn't have a photographic memory, but I remembered the twelve times Joy and I had made love. And the dates.

I remembered the first time, how we sweated for nine days before Joy had her period. I didn't think anything could be worse than waiting for a girl to have her period. I was wrong.

Sitting there on the bed, starting with when Joy was fertile in April and counting off the days, I pinpointed the night in July—the morning, actually— I'd made Joy pregnant. It was the time we'd made love on the pool table in the tavern. 3:00 A.M.

While I filled the coolers, Joy swept the floor. When we finished mopping, she asked, "Can we put some money in the jukebox?"

"Sure, I guess so." I reached behind the jukebox and turned the volume down. "I don't want the music to wake my mom." I gave Joy two red-painted quarters from the music jar behind the bar. "Play something slow. I've got to put the broom and dustpan away."

When I came back, Patsy Cline was singing "You Belong to Me." She's country-and-western, definitely not my favorite music, but that's the stuff Mom had on the jukebox; it's what her customers liked.

"I don't know any of these singers or songs," Joy said.

"That's all right. The one you played is slow."

I went around and pulled the string on the fluorescent ceiling lights, leaving Joy and me bathed in the white, red, yellow, and blue glow of beer-sign lights. I pulled her to me and kissed her. She smelled of perfume, a fragrance that overpowered the tavern smells of stale beer and cigarette/cigar smoke. Our feet barely moved to the music.

When the song died, an impish smile curved Joy's lips. "Want to play pool?"

"Um . . . we better not. Too much noise. Sometimes the balls get stuck. You have to pick up the end of the table to make them roll."

Joy laughed. "I didn't mean regular pool with pool balls."

I thought a moment before grinning. "You mean . . . make love on the pool table?"

She nodded.

"My car's outside," I said.

"There's never enough room."

"The pool table? Are you sure?"

"Yes."

"All right," I said. "The pool table. God, this will ruin my pool game forever." A cord tied in a bow held up Joy's sweatpants. I pulled the cord; the bow released, and her sweatpants dropped to the floor. She wore lemon-yellow bikini panties. Trembling, we made love on the green felt table. . . .

When it was over, I was lost somewhere, floating in another world until Joy hugged me tighter.

"It'll be tough to let go in September," I said, and kissed her.

"I know, but we'll have these memories."

"We'll still be friends, won't we?" I asked.

"Best friends," she assured me.

For a long while, we lay together quietly, still joined. Then we both heard it at the same time: a clunk—not one but two clunks—then the rumbling of two or three pool balls rolling under us, rolling down the track, each ball clicking against the ball ahead of it. Right away I recognized the noise. Joy didn't. Frantic, she pushed me off her and scrambled to sit up. "What's that? I felt something—heard something under us!"

I started laughing. "Pool balls rolling down. They must have been stuck—we shook 'em up." Swinging around, I sat up and let my legs dangle over the edge of the table. Joy spun on her butt and sat beside me, her legs dangling alongside mine in the mellow glow of the beer-sign lights. Joy tweaked me in the ribs. "Stop laughing at me!"

"You're always laughing at me!" I said. "You didn't know what that was, did you? You thought it was a rat or something."

"You're the rat."

"You should've seen your eyes, how big they got."

"If you're going to make fun of me, I'm getting dressed."

"Hey, don't—"

"Too late for apologies." Hopping off the pool table, Joy snatched her clothes from the floor and glided into the women's rest room.

I stood up to gather my clothes from the floor and for the first time realized the condom I had been wearing was gone. A disappearing act. For a moment I couldn't imagine what had happened. Had I forgotten to roll it on? No. I looked on the pool table. I don't know why I expected to find it there. Nothing. I heard the toilet flush.

As I was zipping my jeans, Joy came out of the rest room dressed in her sweatpants and T-shirt. I looked at her, but I wasn't laughing.

"Something happened," I said.

"I know. I found it."

"You found it?"

She threw her head back, and now it was her turn to laugh. "Where did you think it would be?"

"I don't know. I couldn't imagine." I shrugged. "Um, was it still . . . full? I mean, did it empty inside you?"

"God, Jeremy, I don't know. I flushed it down the toilet." She snuggled into my arms. "It's going to be OK, don't worry." But I was thinking of something I'd read after the first time we'd done it, read during my first scare: the male provides 200 to 300 million sperm with each ejaculation. Injected into the female, sperm can stay alive and active for two or three days. It takes only one sperm to fertilize an egg.

What terrible odds.

Joy put her hands on my shoulders, and I held her waist. The walk-in cooler clicked in and started humming in the background. "We're a good team, Jeremy. We're lucky. Nothing's going to happen to us."

I touched her lips with my fingertips. "I hope you're right."

"I am. You'll see."

The comfort and warmth of Joy in my arms quickly crowded out my fears. We were in our own world, having fun, hurting no one. I was sure nothing could destroy our happiness.

Chapter
21

WHEN MOM OPENED MY BEDROOM DOOR, SHE FOUND me sitting on the bed with the *Playboy* calendar in my hands. I could imagine what she suspected I was doing. It didn't matter. Reality was worse than anything she could have suspected. In fact, reality was bizarre. Think about it: rolling pool balls had frightened Joy and forced me to pull out carelessly. Result: spilled sperm. Joy was pregnant, and our world was unraveling.

"You could have knocked," I said.

"You're usually working at the computer. And the door's usually open."

Sighing, I tossed the calendar on the bed. "Well, I wasn't doing what you think."

"Do you want to talk, Jeremy? I heard you on the phone this morning. Remember?"

"What do we have to talk about, Mom?" I fell back and looked at the ceiling. "When have you ever told me about things going on in your life? I hardly know who you are."

"Jeremy, that's not true. Besides, it's not easy explaining things you wish hadn't happened, or you wish you hadn't done. Especially, it's not easy explaining to a child."

"Mom, I am *not* a child." I sat up.

"I meant explain to one of your children." Mom came in and sat in the swivel chair at my desk, where the computer sat. Behind the desk on the wall in eight-by-eleven frames, I'd hung pictures of the USS *New Jersey*, a battleship, and the USS *Constellation*, a carrier—ships my dad had been on. A family picture of Mom, Dad, and me also hung on the wall. I was two and dressed in a little white shirt and blue shorts with suspenders. Dad was tall with thinning hair, but he had grown a thick black mustache.

"Is it Joy?" Mom said. "You've let yourself fall in love with her, haven't you? And you don't know how to tell Darin."

"Give it up, Mom." It suddenly occurred to me that our baby, Joy's baby and mine, might never know much about me, just as I didn't know much about my dad. When the baby was born, I'd be in a navy school or at sea. What if something happened to me? What if I was killed in an accident or killed in a war? My dad was blown away without any warning. That could happen to me. The baby would grow up just like me: never knowing its dad. I couldn't let that happen.

"You're only eighteen. . . ." Mom was saying.

"Well, you can die with your secrets," I said. "September fifth I'm out of here. No one in this town will see me again." That was a lie, of course. I'd always want to see Joy and the baby. Mom, too.

My lie created unexpected results, though: it rattled Mom's cage. She caught her breath and stood up. "Jeremy, don't *say* that."

"It's what you did, isn't it: left home, never went back?" Suddenly I didn't want any more of this conversation. We'd been through hundreds of its variations. She wasn't going to tell me anything, and I had other things on my mind. I looked at my watch. Nearly twelve. I wasn't hungry, but I should eat. Later, I needed to collect my route. This was my last month to get my customers' accounts up-to-date before I handed the route to my replacement.

Mom stood at my bedroom window, holding the curtain back, looking down at Main Street. I got up and headed for the kitchen. I'll never forget Mom's words: "My mother started as a prostitute," she said.

I halted in the doorway, frozen a second. I swung around. "What?"

Her back to me, Mom was still looking out the window. "My mother, your grandmother, was a prostitute."

My mind went blank. "Does that mean—?" I didn't know what I wanted to ask.

Mom turned to look at me. Her eyes were clear. "Does that mean I'm the daughter of some unknown john off the streets of Philadelphia who happened to have enough money? That you're his grandson?"

I swallowed. "Yeah, I guess that's what I mean."

"It's not quite like that." Mom's eyes studied my face carefully. I must've looked confused, shocked, dismayed. Everything. "Are you sure you can handle this?" she said.

Even if her revelation was more than I had bargained for, I couldn't tell her no: I'd bugged her too many times for answers about the past.

"I can handle whatever you have to say," I told her.

Mom smiled crookedly. "I could use a drink." She squeezed her hands together. "Maybe something to eat will do. Are you hungry?"

"Yeah. Sure."

Moving quickly from the fridge to the stove, Mom started making cheeseburgers. I got silverware from the drawer and paper plates from the cupboard. Mom talked all the while. I listened, fascinated at first. Mom was painting a picture on a wall in my mind that had been blank all my life.

"My mother—Lily was her name," Mom said, "wasn't a street hooker doing drugs. She was high class; she worked for an escort service in a day when escort services served an elite clientele. When she was twenty-five, a wealthy Philadelphia lawyer fell in love with her. He was much older. He already had a family. Three kids. He put Mom up in a fancy town house, gave her everything: a car, clothes, jewelry. But within a year she found her days were long and boring. She wanted more—a baby—and threatened to leave him. He finally agreed to have a child. That baby was me."

Mom flipped the sizzling burgers in the pan, and their aroma spread through the kitchen.

"Did you know him? Did you meet him?"

"I knew him. He visited two or three times a month, staying overnight when he could, but we never saw him at Easter or Thanksgiving or Christmas. He reserved those days for family. His *real* family." Bitterness tainted Mom's words. "These are almost done. You got catsup and mustard out?"

"Yes."

"There's fresh lettuce in the crisper. Get that, too."

"Sure."

"And a tomato."

I put the lettuce and tomato on the table.

"So what happened?" I asked. "How long did it last?"

"Twenty years."

"His wife and kids, they never found out?"

"I don't think so. Not while he was alive, anyway."

"What kind of life could you have had?"

"Dismal, most of the time. I felt lonely, left out, confused, unloved. I knew my father had another family, one more important to him. I think my mother loved him, and she stayed with him because she knew it was the best she could do for me and herself. Of course, I never talked about my family to others, never had kids over. I celebrated my birthdays and holidays with just my mother."

"So you went to grade school and high school?"

"Private schools. The best."

"He must have loved you to hang in there for all that time and to spend all that money."

"I suppose he did. I loved music and dance; I was in all my high school productions. When I was a senior, I played Maria in *West Side Story*. He came to see me. After graduation—I was eighteen—I went to New York to study theater, acting, dancing. He was paying for it all. That winter he died unexpectedly. Heart attack. And the money, the support was suddenly gone."

"He didn't leave anything?"

"There was supposed to be a huge bank account and stock and bonds and securities. I don't know if he lied or if his wife found out and tied everything up in court. When Mom called to tell me he was dead, I wanted to quit school and come home. She said no; she'd work things out. Two months after he died, she died: an overdose of sleeping pills." Mom's eyes turned misty. "I have to believe it was an accident, not suicide. She wouldn't have left me like that."

A catch in my throat, I sat down at the table. "What did you do?"

"I was forced to drop out of school. I had nowhere to go, no family to turn to. You must understand that. I lied about my age. I danced in nightclubs, for parties and stags. I found an agent. He put me on a circuit dancing in Saginaw, Columbus, Peoria, Des Moines."

As soon as she said Peoria, I stiffened. I remembered her telling me about a guy named Tony Rose and her getting a black rose tattoo.

Parties, stages, nightclubs—that meant there must have been many men in Mom's life, and it must've been a rotten life. Then the worst thought of all crossed my mind: maybe the guy in the picture, the dead guy I longed to be part of my life, wasn't my dad at all. Could Mom really know? I stared at the table.

Mom set three cheeseburgers on a plate on the table. They didn't even smell good.

"I never wanted to tell you any of this, Jeremy." Mom sat across from me. "I prayed I'd find the right time, the right words. I did a lot of things I'm sorry for. People can be so judgmental. But I had you, got married—I'm not sorry for any of that."

My head snapped up. My face felt like a hunk of ice. "Had me? Got married? Is that what you said? In that order?"

Mom's face was ashen. "Jeremy—"

"You never told me that before."

Mom wrung her hands. "Jeremy, please try to understand."

"Why didn't you tell me?"

"I couldn't—I couldn't force myself."

"Jerry Logan wasn't my father, was he?" I nearly choked on the words.

"He *loved* you! He was a father to you."

"All these years you lied to me."

"Because I love you, Jeremy." Anguish filled Mom's voice. "I wanted to protect you. I'd messed everything else up so bad. I wanted you to have a father."

"That's why you married him?"

"No! We loved each other. He loved you. All that

had happened to me in the past didn't matter to him."

"It matters to me." I stood up, pushing my chair back. "Do you even know who my father is?"

"Jeremy, don't you dare walk out of this house! You have no right to judge me! I've done the best for you I could. Jeremy—!"

I walked out anyway, slamming the door.

Chapter

22

I STOOD IN THE SHADE OF A PINE TREE AND STARED at the small square gravestone in the ground that marked the burial spot of Jerry Logan. The sky was clear, the sun boiling.

I wished I could remember something about Jerry Logan. As always, when I thought about him, my mind drew a blank. What did it matter if I remembered him? He wasn't my father. Why should his death matter to me? In fact, what did it matter if I knew who my father was? Not knowing wasn't a devastating blow. I was alive, wasn't I? That's what counted. The important thing is what a person does with his life, not who his father and mother are.

If Jerry Logan had lived, would Mom and he have told me the truth? I doubted it. I really did.

I knelt down and picked the tall grass around the gravestone that the grass cutter hadn't trimmed. I'll bet Jerry Logan was a neat guy. I hoped he was. He married an exotic dancer with a kid. Maybe his judgment wasn't too good. I didn't know what to think of Mom. I was surely an accident. I wondered why she hadn't gotten an abortion.

Sitting under the pine, I picked up a cone and broke it into pieces. I looked up and saw Joy driving her Mom's Escort slowly down the winding lane leading into the cemetery. My watch said four o'clock. Right on time. I'd been sitting in this cemetery since one o'clock, thinking, watching the ground squirrels scurry from hole to hole and listening to crows caw and blue jays squawk.

Joy parked the Escort behind my car on the gravel lane. She got out and headed toward me, winding her way around the tombstones. She wore a pretty light blue dress and flat shoes; her legs were bare. Her hair fell over her shoulders in loose curls. Where had she been? An abortion clinic in Riverbend?

Standing up, I brushed the pine needles off the seat of my pants. She stopped in front of me, and I wanted to take her hands in mine and kiss her. I smiled instead. "Hi."

She allowed herself a faint smile. "Hi."

"How'd the rest of practice go this morning?"

"Not bad. I'll handle things."

"What did you tell your dad in the parking lot?"

"The same thing you told Darin: I was looking for an aspirin. Funny, we both told the same lie."

"Your dad believe you?"

"I think so."

"Darin didn't. I told him you had a headache; you said your shoulder hurt. I'm positive he doesn't trust us."

"Well . . . we can't blame him, can we?"

"He asked me this morning if we had sex, and I told him we hadn't, but I'm sure he doesn't believe that, either."

Joy nodded and looked at the ground, her blond hair beautiful with the sun on it. "Been waiting long?"

I shrugged and glanced at Jerry Logan's grave. "No, not really." I decided not to tell her the story. That would mean telling her about Mom and everything else. I wasn't ready for that. Maybe some other time.

"Where have you been?" I said. "Joy Kelley doesn't dress up on a hot afternoon for nothing."

"Riverbend."

"Riverbend? To scout the Falcons?" I asked, joking, not wanting to face the thought she'd probably checked out an abortion clinic. An abortion would be the simplest way out of this mess.

Joy shook her head, then looked at the ground again. "I went to a maternal health clinic."

"Maternal health?"

"A place where they provide services for women."

"Not an abortion clinic?"

She frowned. "No."

I took a step toward her. "I'm glad . . . really glad." Joy backed away, apparently afraid I was going to gather her into my arms. I halted. "What did they tell you?"

"I'm pregnant."

I smiled. "I guess we both knew that. What else did they say? Can you play ball?"

"I can during the first trimester. I can continue with any activities I'm already doing, as long as I don't do anything more strenuous than I'm doing now."

"Did they give you something for morning sickness?"

"No. They don't want to give me a drug because taking drugs is like drugging the baby."

"You just have to suffer through the sickness?"

She nodded.

"Games are in the afternoon and at night," she said. "I'll be OK."

"Anyone recognize you? I mean, from your picture in the paper?"

She shook her head. "They were busy. They

examined me and said I was in great shape. The due date's next March." She paused, watching for my reaction.

I hadn't thought about when the baby would be born. "March—that's when you should be in training for your freshman season in college."

"Right."

"Joy, I'm so sorry."

She pushed a wisp of blond hair back from her forehead, and her eyes began filling with tears. "It's not your fault. It's nobody's fault. We were careful. Just not careful enough."

"You know when it happened? You remember the night at the Uptown?"

Joy rubbed the tears out of her eyes with her fingertips. "The pool table?"

"The rolling pool balls," I said ruefully. "What made you go to maternal health?"

"You did. Your buying that pregnancy-test kit. I'll admit it: I didn't want to face the fact I was pregnant. I kept thinking if I could deny it hard enough, it wouldn't be true."

"I figured that."

"Once I was sure I was pregnant, I got to thinking I should find out if it was OK if I pitched. I mean what's more important, a state tournament or a baby?"

"You didn't think about abortion?"

"For only a second."

Joy brushed her hair back again, and this time the sun glinted off Darin's ring circling her wedding-ring finger; it was a slender gold ring with a sparkly diamond.

"Want to sit down?" I asked. "Got our blanket in the car. I'll lay it on the ground." I couldn't believe how calmly Joy and I were talking, how rationally. Finding out the truth lifted a lot of pressure off her. I know it lifted a ton off me. Certainly knowing the truth made deciding what to do next easier. "I'll get the blanket."

"No, Jeremy."

"It's no problem." The blanket was the one we always used to cover ourselves in the backseat of the car, as if we were making out under a tent. Maybe that's why she didn't want me to get the blanket: it would remind her. I started for the car anyway.

"I've got to go," she said.

Cawing in alarm, a crow flew from a tall tombstone with a cross on top. I stopped and turned. "You can't go. There's lots more to talk about."

Tears came back to her eyes. "Just one more thing," she said.

"More than one," I said. "I want you to know I'm going to stand by you through this whole thing. I mean, maybe you and I'll never get married, but I'm going to be here for you anyway. Always."

"Jeremy—"

"I love you, Joy." Again, I took a step toward her, and she backed up against the pine tree. She was backing up all the time, afraid to let me touch her. "I'll help you tell your parents. You decide when. They should probably know first. Then we have to figure out how to tell Darin. I'll worry about my mom."

"We're not telling Darin," she said calmly. She was looking right at me.

I smiled, as if she were joking. "What are you going to do? Run away and hide? In a few months we'll have to tell him something."

She said, "He'll think the baby's his."

Her words stunned me. My eyes snapped open wide, and my jaw dropped. What I was thinking had to be wrong, *had* to be. My face felt as if it were cast in marble—like one of the tombstones in the cemetery—and I couldn't blink or speak for a moment. "You mean . . . you . . . ? You and Darin have . . . ?"

"Not yet—"

"Not *yet?*"

She backed away from the pine tree, and I stalked her.

"Not *yet?* Then you're saying—?"

She wrung her hands. "Darin has to think the baby is his. He *has* to. You don't understand."

Still backing up, she tripped over a tombstone sunk in the ground, Jerry Logan's stone. I grabbed her by the shoulders before she fell. "I'll tell you what I do understand. I understand our thinking we could play with sex all summer and not get burned was stupid, but what you're thinking now is not only stupid—it's *crazy!* It's the worst idea you've ever had."

"You don't understand," she repeated slowly. "I owe Darin."

"Not that much."

"Yes, I do. He has to think the baby is his."

"Why? Because you were his girlfriend before all this started? I understand that. I also understand if Darin's going to think the baby's his, you and he will have to . . ."—I couldn't say it, didn't want to think about it—". . . if you haven't already."

"We haven't, I told you. Jeremy, listen to me—"

I squeezed her shoulders. "No, you listen to me. I love you, Joy Kelley. And I know you love me."

"Jeremy, you're hurting me!" She wrenched free of my grasp.

"Know what else I understand?" I didn't wait for an answer. "I understand a kid has the right to know who his father is." My voice was getting louder, and I couldn't stop it. "You see that tombstone you tripped over?" I pointed at it. "Until today I thought that guy in the ground was my father. A kid has the right to know who his father is!" I shouted the last words at her. Tears burst out of her eyes and rolled down her cheeks. "I have the *right* to let our kid know who I am!"

She was trembling. "Jeremy, let me explain something about Darin and me, something that I've never told you."

But I wasn't listening. What she intended to do blew my mind. No way could she justify it. "This is going to be a screw-*both*-your-buddies summer for you, isn't it?"

She slapped me. Or was it *punched?* It was a punch. It was a roundhouse right. The blow practically ripped my head off and nearly set me on my butt, sprawling among the tombstones. Worse than the blow was the ice in her blue eyes. Face twisted into an ugly mask, lips pulled back, she shrieked, *"I hate you, Jeremy Logan!"*

The side of my face felt like a flaming torch. "J-Joy . . ." Before the sounds barely escaped my lips, she was running for her car, dodging tombstones, leaping the ones in the ground, her light blue skirt flying high on her legs. The Escort roared to life. She drove the gravel lane circling the cemetery like a race-car driver, tires clawing gravel, the car skidding onto the highway.

I stood helplessly over Jerry Logan's stone, my arms hanging limply by my sides, my left cheek throbbing. I needed a cool breeze; there was none. Through blurry eyes, I looked down at Jerry's tombstone. Even though he wasn't my father, I wished he were here. I needed to ask him a question: *What do I do next?*

Chapter
23

I sat at the kitchen table. It was 2:30 a.m. Mom had just closed the Uptown and I heard the stairs creaking. Then the stairway door squeaked open. As she closed it, her hand moved toward the light switch, and I said, "Please don't turn the lights on."

She gave a startled little gasp, her hand flying to her chest. "Jeremy, is that you?"

"Yes."

"God, you scared me half to death."

"Sorry."

"What's wrong? Why don't you want the light on?"

"I like the dark." The dark hid the welt on my left cheek below my eye.

"Are you all right?"

I didn't know how to answer honestly. "I guess I'm all right. Nothing physical is broken."

Mom walked toward the table, passing through a shaft of moonlight streaming through the kitchen window. "A broken heart?"

"You could say that."

She stood next to me, smelling of tavern smoke. "You want to tell me about it?"

"No."

"Your cheeseburgers are in the fridge. Have you eaten?"

"I'm not hungry."

"You should eat something."

"Later maybe."

Pulling out a chair, Mom sat across from me. This was exactly where we'd sat when we'd parted over fourteen hours before. I'd learned a lot since then. I'd learned there were events in life over which one had no control, and that it was easy to screw up the events over which one did have control. That combination made the potential for disaster in life staggering. Probably 70–30 in favor of disaster.

I rubbed the top of the table with my fingertips. "I'm sorry about yelling at you this afternoon." My voice was a whisper. "You were right: I had no right to judge you. I'm sorry."

"You've been sitting here in the dark, waiting to tell me that?"

"I tried sleeping, but I couldn't. I had to tell you sometime."

"Oh, God, Jeremy. *I'm* the one who's sorry. And ashamed. Sorry I could never find the right way to tell you about my life, ashamed that I couldn't tell you *better* things about me. I've struggled so long to do the right thing. Sometimes you can't find the right thing. There isn't any."

I couldn't see Mom's eyes in the darkness, but the waver in her voice told me she was nearly crying.

"It's all right," I said. "I understand. I understand a lot more than you think." I paused and inhaled. "I just wondered . . . you know, do you know who my father is?" That seemed like a terrible question to ask my mother, but I had to.

She was sniffling. She got up and went to the cupboard to get a Kleenex from the box by the toaster. Sitting at the table again, she dabbed at her eyes. "I was never a hooker, Jeremy. . . ." Her voice caught. "God, it's hard to talk to your son about stuff like this."

"Mom, you don't have to tell me the details. I just wondered, you know, who my father is."

"Frank Kitzmann, a Des Moines businessman." Mom's fingers picked at the Kleenex, tearing it into tiny bits. "He came into Tuxedo's nearly every night, a place where I worked. He gave great tips. . . ."

I squirmed in my chair. "Mom, I don't care about details."

She blew her nose into a bit of Kleenex she hadn't shredded. "Frank and I started seeing each other," she went on. "I got pregnant. I swear I was careful—always careful—but . . . it happens, you know. It just happens. . . ."

I can relate, Mom.

"When I told Frank, I thought maybe he would put me up like the Philadelphia lawyer put my mom up. That didn't happen."

"Was he married?"

"Yes," Mom said. "And he wanted nothing more to do with me. He gave me cash for an abortion and enough to get out of town. At Tuxedo's, dating customers was against the rules. He conveniently told another dancer. She squealed, and the day after I told Frank I was pregnant, I was fired. The dancer and Frank planned it, I'm sure. So there I was: a dancer, no job, and pregnant. Enter Jerry Logan into my life."

"Did you know him? I mean before that?"

"I hadn't met him, but I'd seen him. He was a beer-truck driver. He delivered at Tuxedo's in the afternoons and often stayed to watch for a while when we did shows for the foundry workers getting off at three. The day I got fired he spotted me that afternoon in a downtown bar. He talked to me for a while. I cried on his shoulder, told him about Frank Kitzmann, that I'd lost my job, told him about the fix I was in. Jerry made me promise to wait for him till he got off work. He came back at six and took me home with him. He said I could stay till I figured out what I wanted to do. He was a bachelor, an ex-sailor from Oregon, never married, lonely.

"I wanted a place to settle in. I was so tired of drifting. I put off getting an abortion. Jerry never asked me to move out. I found a job in a restaurant. I worked as long as I could. You were born. Jerry and I got married. He adopted you. All three of us clicked. He'd saved some money. Tavern work was what we both knew. We moved to Maple Grove and made a down payment on the Uptown. I'd never been happier." Mom's voice trailed off.

I slumped back in my chair.

"Now you know, Jeremy. Do you hate me?"

"No. I'm a little numb, maybe. But I don't hate you. This . . . this Frank Kitzmann, is he still alive?"

"I don't know. He would be . . . in his seventies, I suppose."

"He never tried to inquire about me?"

"I'm sure he thinks I had an abortion. If you found him and asked him about me, I doubt that he'd remember. I was probably one of many. Are you going to look for him?"

"No. There's no point, really. I . . . well, thanks

for telling me." I cleared my throat. "Um . . . you want to know something about me . . . what's going on in my life?"

Mom nodded. "I'd like very much to know what's going on . . . and help, if I can."

"I wasn't going to tell you this . . . not right away, at least, but I might as well. What you just told me . . . I have something difficult to tell, too."

I laid out the triangle of Darin, Joy, and me, beginning with the night of the prom. I mean, I didn't tell her every detail—only that Joy and I became involved the night of the prom, that she was pregnant, and that she had decided to con Darin into thinking the baby was his.

"Oh, Jeremy . . . Jeremy," Mom kept saying. "Oh, Jeremy . . ."

I felt my eyes getting watery. "After the tournament," I said when I was finishing, "I'm going to tell Darin the truth." I stood. "I don't care what happens. A kid has the right to know his father."

"Why does Joy want to lie to Darin?"

I rattled off the reasons I could think of: "She doesn't want him to know we betrayed him; she feels obligated; she was his girlfriend before all this started. He's in a wheelchair; he's lost everything else; loyalty comes first; Darin might do something stupid to himself if he finds out the truth."

"Would he?"

"I don't know." I started to pace the kitchen. "He might. His dad thinks he's manic-depressive."

"Are you sure Joy loves you?"

"I'd bet on it."

"How would the two of you manage with a baby?"

"I don't know." I let out a long sigh. "Darin's parents have lots of money. They might be happy to raise a grandchild. Darin and Joy could get married, then go off to school together, and the baby would be just fine with them. All problems solved."

"Maybe that's why Joy wants Darin to think the baby is his."

"But it's *not*, and Joy doesn't love Darin."

"What will happen if you tell everyone the truth? Have you thought of that?"

"Are you saying I should go along with Joy's lie?"

"No. But you need to be prepared for the consequences. What will happen?"

"Well . . ." I bit my lip and thought a moment. "Darin and Joy will hate me forever. Maybe Darin will kill himself. That will be on my conscience for the rest of my life. Or maybe Darin will forgive Joy, and they'll get married. Or maybe Joy will put the baby up for adoption—that would be the easy thing to do—and start school a year late. I'll never get to see the baby or be part of its life." That thought startled me. "I don't have any say about adoption, do I?"

"I don't think so."

"I have to talk to Joy again. She has to understand a kid has a right to know its father."

"She didn't ask for this child, Jeremy. Marrying Darin or putting the baby up for adoption would allow her to go to college and play ball. Which is apparently what she wants to do."

"Both choices leave me out."

"You said if you tell the truth, she'll hate you. You'll be left out anyway."

I stopped pacing and looked at the ceiling, shaking my head. "God, I'd give *anything* if things could go back to the way they were. I mean, to when Darin and Joy and I were just friends. I feel as if I'm trapped in a nightmare. I can't escape."

Mom stood, faced me, and we hugged each other, awkwardly at first because we hadn't hugged in years.

The digital clock radio on top of the fridge blinked 4:00 A.M. "I've got to clean the tavern and deliver papers," I said.

"God, we've been talking for a long time. It's the most time we've spent together in a long while." She kissed me on the cheek, then pulled back, alarmed. "There's a lump under your eye."

"I said something to Joy this afternoon I shouldn't have. She got mad and tagged me."

Mom said, "Maybe in a day or two, after you

think about things, the two of you will be able to talk more calmly."

"I hope so. Good night, Mom."

I felt good about what happened between Mom and me that morning, the way we'd talked. I'd never felt closer to her, and telling her my secret had lightened the weight on my shoulders. I couldn't wait to tell the rest of the world.

Chapter
24

EIGHT TEAMS OPENED PLAY IN THE STATE TOURNA-
ment on Monday in Riverbend, the other eight playing Tuesday night. Maple Grove landed in the
Tuesday bracket, taking on Clear Creek in a
6:30 P.M. contest.

During the pregame warm-ups, I sat in a lawn
chair behind the chain-link fence at third base, next
to the Leafs' dugout. I balanced a clipboard on each
knee, one with a game book, the other with a pitching
chart.

I knew instantly Joy was in trouble. During the
warm-up, she bounced two pitches to the backstop
and threw another over Lucas's head. When she
faced the top of the Clear Creek batting order in the
first inning, she walked the bases loaded without

retiring a hitter. During that stretch, she threw sixteen pitches, ten of them balls. Her pitches lacked
velocity, and she seemed to be releasing the ball differently. I couldn't tell why. I was so nervous I could
hardly hold my pencil, and I started to chew my
bottom lip.

"C'mon, Joy. You can do it, babe. Throw strikes."

A tiny school in the northeast part of the state,
Clear Creek sported a fancy 34–2 record but wasn't
ranked high in the state because it played dinky
schools. So a bit of mystery surrounded the Clear
Creek Tigers: either they were a poor team with a
flashy record, or they were a vastly underrated team
with a flashy record.

Then the Tigers' cleanup hitter tagged one of Joy's
fastballs but lifted it too high. The Leafs' center
fielder, Bev Davis, camped under it. Tagging up at
third, the runner trotted home after the catch for a
1–0 lead. Dressed in orange and black, Tiger fans
went wild in the stands. I shifted in my chair.

"C'mon, Joy. Strikes, babe."

I'd thought about not coming to any of the tournament games. I had a feeling something like this
might happen. Joy would get off to a shaky start,
and we'd lose the very first game. The defeat would
shatter everyone's dream of a state title for Maple
Grove and Joy's dream of a scholarship to Iowa. By
not coming, I could avoid witnessing the agony. Be-

sides, I wouldn't have to see Darin and try to talk to him, wondering if he and Joy were making it. I hadn't heard from him or Joy since Saturday. But the truth was I simply couldn't stay away from Joy's games. I wanted her to win so badly I could taste it. She deserved to win. I wanted to chart every pitch and do anything I could to help her.

With runners moving, Clear Creek's number-five hitter took a hefty swing but topped one of Joy's fastballs and grounded out to second, both runners advancing. Two outs, runners on second and third— I'd seen Joy pitch herself out of tougher situations than this. When she was on.

"C'mon, Joy!"

Watching the game without Darin next to me was strange. I'd taken him to all of Joy's other games this season. He always called me or I called him. Not this time, though.

The next batter belted Joy's first pitch past Corky Robinson at third, a screaming line drive that rolled to the left-field corner. I leapt out of my chair. "Second!" I screamed. "Throw the ball to second!" Both Tiger runners raced home, and the throw from Tobie Shepherd in left was too late. The batter slid into second under Suzie Stiles's tag with a double. The Clear Creek dugout went crazy, screaming and cheering. The Tigers led 3–0, and Joy had retired only one hitter. My shoulders sagged.

Coach Thorton walked slowly to the mound, head down, kicking at the dirt as he walked. He blocked my vision, so I couldn't see the reaction on Joy's face as he stood there talking to her, first wagging his head sideways, then nodding up and down. Shock rippled through me when he turned away from Joy; he held the ball in his hand. I couldn't believe it. Thorton waved for Annie Meyer to come out of the dugout and take her warm-up pitches. Joy was out of the game. She'd pitched one-third of an inning, and had given up three runs on one hit and three walks. My heart dropped to my heels.

Joy sprinted off the mound. Stomping into the dugout, she threw her glove against the wall as the other players ducked. She plunked down alone at the end of the bench; everyone stayed away from her. She sat with her elbows on her knees, her hands over her face. I knew she must be crying.

I was so stunned I didn't realize Mrs. Steele had rolled Darin up next to me in his chair. Avoiding Darin's eyes, I looked over my shoulder at Mrs. Steele and said, "Hi." I didn't want to look into her eyes, either, but that was the easier choice.

"Hello." She smiled back, then added sheepishly, "I tried to get here on time."

"I kept telling her it was a six-thirty game," Darin said. "But she wouldn't get out of the pool."

"Where's Mr. Steele?" I asked.

"Parking the van. He let us out at the gate."

Mrs. Steele looked at me. "What happened to your cheek?"

My fingers touched what remained of the black-and-blue welt below my eye. "Nothing. It's . . . a bee sting."

"Why didn't you call?" Darin asked.

I looked at him, dismayed.

"Why didn't *you* call?" I asked. "You're the one who's mad, remember?"

"I think I'll watch from the bleachers," Mrs. Steele said. "It's so hot standing here." She took off.

"You could've called," Darin said. "I *hate* having my parents taking me places as if I were a kid."

"I'm the one who's making it with your girlfriend, remember? Why would I want to call you? Why would you even want to talk to me?"

"Forget that. I know you're not making it with Joy."

"How do you know? She tell you that?"

"Yeah, she told me. I asked her. She said you weren't man enough, old buddy."

"She said that?"

"She couldn't stop laughing at the thought of you making it with her. I should've known you weren't man enough."

I wanted to say, *Laugh at this, buddy: I got her pregnant!* But I held back the words and clenched my teeth. He'd find out soon enough.

"Batter up!" yelled the umpire.

I turned to the game. Left-hander Annie Meyer stepped to the mound, ready to fire for the Maple Leafs.

"What's happening?" Darin asked. "Where's Joy?"

"Look at the scoreboard." I scribbled Annie's name into the score book. "Joy got belted out of the game."

"Three–zip!" Darin said. "Oh, God—"

"She couldn't throw strikes. When she did, they blasted her. Something's wrong with her release."

"She's got a bruised hand, a jammed thumb."

"What?"

"A bruised hand," Darin repeated. "Jammed thumb. She can't grip the ball right. Of all the stupid things! She says she slipped in the shower."

Oh, no!

She hadn't slipped in the shower: she'd hit me with a roundhouse right high on my cheek, her thumb in the way. "Have they tried the whirlpool?"

"They had her hand in the whirlpool three or four times Sunday and Monday. Today, too. Said it might take another day before she's ready, but she said she wanted to pitch today."

I swallowed. If ever a team needed a sophomore for a heroine, the Leafs needed Annie Meyer. And so did I. Built like a bulldozer, Annie walked the first batter she faced but struck out the Tigers' number-eight and -nine hitters, ending the inning quickly.

Wow!

I sighed in relief, and Darin said, "Wait till she gets to the heart of the lineup. Then we'll see what she's got."

"She'll be all right."

C'mon, Annie!

The Leafs picked up a run of their own in the first on an error. "If Annie can hold these guys," I said after the first inning, "I'm sure we can catch them. Their pitcher throws junk. After our guys see her for a couple of innings, they'll have her timed. They'll tag her."

"Big 'if,' " Darin said.

When Annie gave up a run in the fourth to make the score 4–1, I started to worry again. Shifting back and forth in my chair, I kept thinking that if we lost this game it would be my fault: I'd done everything I could to hurt Joy and to jeopardize the Leafs' championship drive.

In the bottom half of the fifth, the Leafs went to work. They batted around, with Corky Robinson's thundering bases-loaded homer putting them in front 5–4. The Tigers changed pitchers, but Suzie and Annie jumped on her for consecutive singles. With two outs, Tosha Williams tripled off the fence in right field, giving the Maple Leafs a 7–4 lead. They never looked back. When Annie struck out the Tigers' final hitter in the top of the seventh, our bleachers erupted with wild cheers: "WE'RE NUMBER ONE!" The team members swamped Annie on the mound, and I exhaled loud and long. "Thank God. Thank God."

Even Darin was excited. "We beat the jerks!" he said.

Chapter
25

THE LEAFS' VICTORY OVER CLEAR CREEK VAULTED them into the winners' bracket against Danville Wednesday at 6:30 P.M. I didn't hang around after the Clear Creek game. I didn't want to hear everyone ask Joy about her performance. And what could I say to Joy? "Hurt your hand? That'll teach you to belt me."

When I saw Darin's parents approaching—Darin was talking to a couple of girls—I collected my lawn chair and charts, and I ditched him, heading out of the stadium.

Wednesday morning about nine, Darin called to gripe. "Why'd you take off so early last night? I looked around and all of a sudden you were gone."

"We won. Your parents were there; you didn't need a ride home. There wasn't any other reason for me to hang around. Besides, I wanted to get the stats into the computer."

"You going to give me a ride to the game tonight?"

I hesitated. I'd never refused to take him before. If his parents took him, he'd sit next to me anyway. "All right. I'll drive you."

At the game that evening, while the rest of the team was taking infield and batting practice, Joy came over to the fence where Darin and I sat behind third base. I guessed she wanted to talk to Darin, certainly not me, but I spoke first: "Hi. How you feeling?" She could interpret the question either way: her pregnancy or her hand.

"Fine." She regarded me with cool, indifferent eyes.

"All around?"

"All around," she said.

Darin said, "Then Thorton better stick you in the lineup tonight. You've got to win some games."

"Just as long as the team wins," Joy said. "That's what really matters."

"Like hell. You need that scholarship."

"See you right after the game," Joy said to Darin, smiling at him, snubbing me.

"You bet." Darin's eyes gleamed.

Joy trotted back into the dugout, and I entered the teams' lineups into the score book.

Annie was set to face the Danville Dragons. A big school from the northern part of the state, ranked third with a 40–4 record, the Dragons possessed a tandem of all-state power hitters: Sarah Tuthill and Wendy Saur. I knew Thorton felt he was between a rock and a hard spot. He hated to pitch Annie, who had never faced anyone as tough as the Dragons, and he hated to pitch Joy, whose hand might not be ready. I figured he'd picked Annie because she was healthy, and she'd done a good job against Clear Creek. He'd go with her as long as he could, the entire game if possible. If she faltered, he'd throw Joy to the Dragons.

Her confidence sky-high from yesterday's performance, using a good fastball and a sharp-breaking curve, Annie mowed down the Dragons for three innings. In the bottom of the fourth, they touched her for a run on two walks, an error, and Tuthill's RBI single. Annie escaped the inning leaving three runners on base, trailing 1–0.

"That's all right, Annie!" I yelled at her, as the Leafs trotted off the field. "You're doing great!"

"She'll never last," Darin said. "We need some runs."

"We'll get some runs," I said. "I can feel it. Besides, the longer Annie lasts the better for Joy. Maybe Joy can rest her hand till tomorrow."

"If there is a tomorrow."

"There will be," I said.

I was right about the Leafs scoring runs. Supplying the power, Corky drilled a two-run homer in the top of the fifth with Bev on, Corky's second homer of the tournament. The blast gave Maple Grove a 2–1 lead. Corky was a streak hitter. When she was on a streak, watch out! And she looked as if she were starting one—a homer in the opening game, a homer now. If her streak lasted through the championship game, Maple Grove could never be counted out. If the pitching held up . . .

Annie cruised through the bottom of the fifth but collapsed in the sixth, giving up singles to the first two batters she faced.

"What did I tell you?" Darin growled. "She's not going to last."

"You've got that right." I watched Thorton as he stood by the dugout entrance and motioned for Joy; then he strode to the mound.

"The moment of truth," I said. "Joy's coming in."

"I wish I had a beer," Darin said.

Taking over with a 2–1 lead, two runners on base, no outs, and the Dragons' heavy hitters coming to the plate, Joy had to prove she was ready to pitch. I knew it. Thorton knew it. The rest of our fans knew it. Joy knew it.

She kicked at the mound, vicious kicks, till she'd kicked every atom of dirt into its proper place. Then she took her warm-ups: fastballs, all of them. Good fastballs with pop to them. Over the plate.

"She's ready," I said.

"She better be," Darin answered.

"Play ball!" the umpire yelled. "Batter up!"

While the batter stood at the plate, waving her bat, waiting, Joy slammed the ball into her glove four or five times. Then the batter backed out of the box, looking at her coach on third. "Let's go!" the ump shouted. "Play ball!"

"C'mon, Joy. You can do it, babe."

The batter moved back into the box, tapped her bat on the plate, and hardly had time to bring the bat to her shoulder when Joy fired a fastball—right at her head. My mouth dropped open. Flinging her bat, the batter fell backward to the ground on the seat of her pants, her helmet flying off.

"What the *hell!*" I jumped up.

The Danville bench and fans leapt up and screamed: "Booo! Throw her out! Booooo!"

"Did you see that?" I asked Darin.

"It was close," he said.

I'd never seen Joy throw at anyone. Even if Thorton had told her to throw at a batter, I didn't believe Joy would. I think the embarrassment of being knocked out of yesterday's game and the stress of other frustrations in Joy's life were knotted up in that one pitch. Now that the pitch was out of her system, she was ready to throw strikes. I knew one thing: if Joy threw another near-miss pitch, we'd have a brawl. That's all Joy needed: being pregnant and getting punched in the belly.

As the batter got up and dusted herself off, the ump handed her the helmet. She pulled it over her short brown hair and stepped nervously to the plate. The Dragon fans continued to boo, and their dugout began to chant: "She's wild! She's wild! Take her out! Take her out! Take her out NOW!"

"C'mon, Joy . . . C'mon, babe."

"Throw heat!" Darin yelled.

Joy's second pitch was a fastball. The batter jumped back a mile, but the pitch was a perfect strike, a hummer.

"Strrike!" shouted the ump.

A smile seized my face. "She's on!" I yelled at Darin. "She's on!" I could tell from that one pitch. Her windup and release, her rhythm—she was in tune. Everything was clicking. "The batter didn't even *see* the ball," I said. "Did you hear it pop?"

"I told you she should be in there!" Darin said. "Nobody listens to me."

On two more pitches, Joy fanned the batter for the first out. Suddenly a silence fell over the Dragon fans and their dugout. Stomping in the bleachers, Maple Grove's green-and-white-clad fans began their familiar chant: "We're number one! We're number one!"

"Maybe we are number one," I said as Joy finished the inning, striking out the fearsome duo of Tuthill and Saur. Joy had needed only twelve pitches to polish off three Dragon hitters.

The Leafs failed to score in their half of the seventh, but that didn't matter. In the bottom of the inning, Joy set the Dragons down on strikes again, saving the game 2–1. Six strikeouts in a row. I jumped up and grabbed the chain-link fence. "Way to go, team!" I screamed. "Way to go, Joy!" I didn't think anything could stop the Leafs now!

Before the stands cleared, before Thorton finished his center-field lecture to the girls, I wheeled Darin to the van, loaded him in, and headed home. Happy as I was for Joy and the team, I wasn't hanging around. Darin complained all the way, demanding to know why we were leaving early.

"I have a route to collect. It's eight o'clock. Some people are home only during the evening."

"You are such a *jerk!*" he said bitterly. "Didn't you hear Joy say she'd meet me right after the game?"

"Hey, look! I got things to do. She knows where you live."

When I got Darin home it was eight-thirty, the edge of twilight, the air still warm and muggy. His mother didn't answer the door, so I figured she must be in back by the pool, and I wheeled him around the house. When I'd picked Darin up at five-thirty, Mrs. Steele was wearing a black bikini. I'd carted

Darin away so quickly I'd hardly had time to say "Hello" or "Good-bye."

Now Mrs. Steele was lying on her stomach on a towel by the pool's edge in the shadow of the wooden fence that surrounded the yard. Darin didn't see her, though, because he was trying to crank his head around so he could look at me and yell at me at the same time.

"I don't understand you! Turn this chair around so I can see you."

I whirled Darin around. He was yelling at me, but I wasn't listening.

I was looking past him, at Mrs. Steele, lying on the towel. She was nude. She must have fallen asleep, and the bickering between Darin and me woke her. She raised her head, looked at me, and smiled. I could hardly breathe.

"Are you listening to me?" Darin was saying. "What are you looking at?" He couldn't twist his neck far enough around to see.

"Nothing." My word sounded like a croak.

Mrs. Steele picked up the two pieces of her black bikini and tiptoed quickly into the house.

"I've got to go," I said.

"I'm asking you what the hell's wrong with you? You didn't call to take me to the first game. You don't listen to what I want to do." His eyes became small and cold. "You're jealous of what Joy and me have going despite this chair, aren't you, old buddy? You're trying to get even."

"I'm not jealous," I said. Stepping behind Darin's chair, I whirled him around. "Push yourself into the house. Your mother's probably there. Where's your dad?"

"AA meeting. He goes practically every night. Or some drunk calls him on the phone, needing help."

At that moment, wearing a short robe belted in front, Mrs. Steele slid open the glass doors to the patio and stepped barefoot outside. My guess was she wore nothing under the robe. "Home already? Did we win?"

"Two—one," Darin said.

"Joy finished the last two innings," I added.

"It's about time she did something," Darin said.

"She struck out six in a row," I said. "Two more games and we're state champs."

Mrs. Steele was watching me intently.

"Going to drive me tomorrow?" Darin asked.

"Why should I? I'm tired of fighting with you all the time." I turned.

"Won't you stay, Jeremy?" Mrs. Steele said. "You can help me fix lemonade in the kitchen. The evening's hot, even if the sun is going down."

"I really have to go, Mrs. Steele."

"He's being such a jerk," Darin said.

"We haven't seen much of you the last couple of

days," Mrs. Steele said. "You're always welcome, you know."

"I know." I cleared my throat. "I have to go." I whirled and hurried around the house to my car. Maybe after the tournament was over, my best bet was to get out of town in a hurry. Say nothing. Do nothing. Leave for the navy early, before I got myself into more trouble that I couldn't handle. Forget about everything, everybody. Leave.

Chapter 26

FOUR TEAMS STOOD POISED TO CLAIM THE STATE SOFT-
ball title: in the upper bracket, Riverbend West and
Sioux City Heelan; in the lower bracket, New
Hampton and Maple Grove. The Leafs were the only
small school left.

I talked to Joy before the start of the New Hampton game. Sioux City had taken Riverbend West into
extra innings in the first game at six-thirty, so the
New Hampton–Maple Grove game was a late starter.
I left Darin in his chair at our spot behind third base
and went to the concession stand for popcorn.

In her green-and-white uniform, glove hanging
from her wrist, Joy was buying a Coke. We saw each
other at the same time.

"Hi," I said. "Want some popcorn? Smells good.
Lots of butter."

She shook her head, then sipped her Coke. Fans milled about munching popcorn and hot dogs, licking ice-cream bars.

"I hear you're starting."

"That's right."

I ate a few kernels of popcorn. "Are you ready?"

She smiled a bit. "As ready as I'll ever be."

"You were great yesterday. Six batters, six strike-outs. Forty-five pitches. You were spectacular."

"Thanks."

"Can I ask you something?"

"What?"

"Did you throw at that first batter?"

Joy's grin was sheepish. "No. I was so scared and nervous I could hardly hang onto the ball."

"That's what I thought."

"But after that wild one, I felt OK."

"Um . . . you still feeling OK? I mean . . . you know."

"I'm feeling fine."

"Sick in the morning?"

She gave me a wicked glance, then looked quickly around to see if anyone had heard me. "Jeremy—!"

"I'm sorry," I said. "I'm worried about you, that's all."

"I'm fine. Don't worry about me."

"I'm sorry about what I said the other day. About screwing your buddies. My face paid the price."

"So did my hand."

"Is it better?"

"It's pretty good."

"I'm sorry about your hand, too. Sometimes I'd be better off if I kept my mouth shut."

She shrugged. "Maybe neither one of us was thinking very clearly. I have to go." She started to walk away.

"Joy."

She turned. "What?"

"Um . . . are you and Darin . . . ?"

"What?" she said impatiently.

"Are you . . . ?" I couldn't ask her. Now wasn't the time. Maybe I didn't want to know if they were making love, just as she hadn't wanted to know if she were pregnant. "Good luck," I said. "I want you to win. I really do. I want you to win whatever scholarship you want. That's the truth."

"I don't know what I'd do with a scholarship."

"We'll figure something out."

"I have to go, Jeremy."

After the sun went down, the evening cooled, giving everyone a break from the heat. Screaming fans for both teams filled the stands, and the night air pulsed with tension. Going into the fifth inning under the lights, the New Hampton River Queens and the Maple Leafs were locked in a scoreless duel, with Joy working on a no-hitter. The Queens' pitcher Cheryl Gibson was pitching a great game herself, scattering five hits over five innings, never more than one an inning, walking no one. Joy had walked four. Not bad for her.

In the bottom of the fifth, Joy issued her fifth walk. The runner stole second, and the next hitter followed with a surprise bunt. Corky fielded the ball cleanly on the third-base line but had trouble getting the ball out of her glove, so the throw to first was late—a hit for the batter. Suddenly the Queens had runners on first and third, no outs.

"She'll blow it," Darin said. "I know she will."

"No, she won't," I said. "She's pitching with confidence. I've never seen her look better." Then under my breath: "C'mon, Joy! C'mon, babe!"

When Joy struck out the next two batters, I thought she was home free. Then it happened. With two swinging strikes on her, unable to touch the ball, the Queens' left-handed batter laid a desperation bunt down the first-base line. Both runners took off with the pitch. Joy and first baseman Tosha Williams scrambled after the ball. "Roll foul!" I screamed. But the ball didn't; it was a perfect bunt. Joy fielded the ball, whirled, and without looking fired to first for what should have been the third out, but second baseman Pee Wee Avila wasn't covering first. She had dashed to second to make a play. Meanwhile,

Joy's throw sailed into right field and rolled to the fence. Both runners scored and the batter ended up at third. Suddenly the Leafs trailed 2–0.

I was numb.

"Who was supposed to be covering first?" Darin screamed.

"Avila." Disgusted, I shook my head and watched the electric scoreboard in left field flash the error light. Joy was pitching a one-hitter, yet she was losing.

"Why did she throw it?" Darin said. "Couldn't she see no one was covering?"

"Someone's supposed to be there. It's automatic. Someone's supposed to be there."

"If she wouldn't have thrown it, we'd be only one run behind."

"We're going to be OK," I said. "We can hit their pitcher. All we need to do is bunch a few hits together."

"It's stupid to throw the ball like that when there's no one there."

"Shut up, Darin."

My main concern now was how the two-run deficit would affect Joy's pitching. The Leafs' sloppy play allowing New Hampton to score was the kind of thing that often upset Joy, disrupting her rhythm, making her wild. The Queens still had a runner at third. No way could the Leafs let New Hampton score again and drop behind 3–0.

If I had any doubts about Joy, they were unfounded. Stepping back onto the mound, she struck out the next batter on four pitches and trotted back to the dugout unruffled, though Thorton was quick to corner both Joy and Pee Wee in the dugout, chewing them out furiously.

What I said about the Leafs being able to hit the Queens' pitcher proved to be true. They got to her in the seventh. In that inning our girls took advantage of an error and a walk and bunched together three hits—one of them was Joy's double—to grab a 3–2 lead. Joy set the Queens down in order in their half of the seventh, and the game was history.

I felt emotionally drained. For the second time in three games, the Leafs had come from behind to win. They showed courage and maturity. Maybe Joy showed the most courage and maturity of all. She appeared focused. All the other things happening in her life she'd apparently been able to set aside.

Was she making love with Darin?

"Win or lose," Darin said, "tomorrow night there's going to be some serious partying going on!"

Chapter 27

"TONIGHT'S THE BIG GAME?" MOM ASKED. SHE STOOD at the stove, stirring chili for lunch, the aroma bubbling out of the saucepan.

"The title game against Riverbend West," I said. Though she wasn't into sports, Mom was as happy as anyone else in town for the Leafs. "West beat Joy the last two years in the district tournament," I told her. "This year our district was split: Riverbend went north and the Leafs went west, so now we've both got a chance at the title, two teams from the same conference. Shows you where the power is in the state." I sat at the table, pouring milk into my glass. "Too bad you can't be there."

"Have to work to pay bills. After you leave I'd like to sell this place."

"What would you do?"

"That's it: I don't know. You'd think by the time a person hits their forties they'd have their life figured out." Mom brought two steaming bowls of chili to the table. "Will we win tonight?"

"I think so. West has got speed, experience, good hitters, and a great pitcher—Val Hightower. We don't have much speed and no tournament experience, but when Joy's on she's the best pitcher in the state. She's the equalizer. She was on last night."

"From what her father says about her in the paper, she's the best in the world."

I slurped the hot chili. "He exaggerates a little. Not much. Just a little."

"Have you said anything to Darin about . . . you know?"

"Not yet." I dropped cheddar cheese bits into my chili. "I don't want him yelling at Joy and getting her upset. I'm going to wait till a couple of days after the game, till after everyone's had a chance to celebrate. I don't want to ruin a good celebration. Or make things worse if we lose."

"Are you going to tell Joy your plans?"

"I'll ask her to come with me to tell him. If she won't, I'll do it alone."

Mom spread butter on a cracker. "What if Joy says it's not true?"

"What's not true?"

"What if Joy tells Darin she's not pregnant? You made the story up."

I blinked. I'd never thought of that.

Mom said, "Maybe by the time this tournament is over she'll be sick of both of you. Maybe she'll grab a scholarship, get an abortion, and then go off to college, dumping you *and* Darin."

"She wouldn't have an abortion. I know she wouldn't. No matter what."

"She could still say you were lying."

"Why?"

"A month from now she could tell Darin she was pregnant. The baby's his. She could say the baby was born prematurely. Who would be the wiser?"

"The baby might look like me. There are tests a guy can take to prove he's a father—or isn't."

"You'll be in the navy, Jeremy, perhaps far from here. Tests like that involve lawyers, money, court battles."

I drew in a breath. How many ways could this mess turn out?

"The bottom line is this, Mom: Every kid has the right to know the truth about himself. About his parents. That's what I'm going to fight for. No matter what."

Mom reached across the table and put her hand on mine. "I think you're right, Jeremy. I really do."

———

That afternoon I worked on collecting my route and tried to concentrate on that night's title game. I was already getting nervous about it. Joy had faced the Riverbend West Falcons eight times during the past three years. She was down 3–5 to them, the only team—conference or nonconference—to hold an edge over her.

When I got home from collecting, a brilliant idea flashed in my brain. I immediately went to the computer and spent several hours booting up softball stats. I compiled stats showing what pitches Joy had thrown to the Falcon hitters, whom she struck out, what Falcons hit her, what pitches they nailed, which ones they couldn't handle. I'd been keeping that information in the computer because I liked doing it, and I thought someday Joy would like a pitch-by-pitch printout of the games she'd played. By the time I finished that afternoon, I printed a scouting report of Falcon hitters that major-league statisticians couldn't equal.

Then I called Joy. She answered on the third ring. "Hi. How you doing?"

"What do you want, Jeremy?"

"Got a minute?"

"I'm in a hurry. Thorton wants us at school at five."

"I want to talk softball."

I explained what information I'd compiled and

asked her to get a piece of paper and a pencil. "I'll give you the probable starting Falcon lineup and tell you exactly what pitches the players have hit off you and which ones you've fooled them on."

"Jeremy, Thorton sets up the pitching strategy. He calls all the pitches."

"To hell with Thorton. He thinks like a football coach. Power, that's all he knows. To win this game you'll have to use *all* your pitches. I told you the other day to be effective you don't have to strike out everyone. Shake Thorton off. Throw the drop, curve, change-up."

"Jeremy, I can't unless he says so."

"I'm telling you seventy percent of the balls the Falcons hit off you this season have been fastballs. They're a fastball-hitting team. At exactly the right time, to exactly the right hitters, you need to throw some junk. Keep the batters off stride." I was losing patience. "Get a piece of paper and pencil, will you? A notebook would be better. Get a notebook."

She didn't answer. "Joy, I'm trying to help you." Now I was half mad. "Look, I'll give the same notes to Thorton. You and he can decide what to do, but you should have a chance to study them before the game. OK?"

No answer.

"Joy, get a notebook."

"All right."

She was gone a moment, then came back. "Got it?" I asked.

"Yes."

"All right. Here we go." I dictated every scrap of information I had, then said, "Study that before the game. Take the notebook into the dugout with you and look at it between innings. It could make the difference between your winning and losing, your being a state champ or runner-up." Again she didn't answer. "Are you listening to me?"

"Yes . . . Jeremy . . . ?"

"What?"

"I appreciate this."

"Hey, I'm your biggest fan. I'd do anything for you to win." I paused a moment. "Well . . . good luck."

"Thanks."

Game night was a soft summer night with temperatures in the mid-seventies, a light breeze blowing to straight-away center field. The American flag on a pole beyond center field occasionally inhaled enough breeze to wave itself. I brought Darin to the game early and left him with a bunch of senior high girls he knew. They could push him around for a while.

I spotted Thorton standing at the fence behind the plate, watching the Falcons take batting practice.

I walked up to him and gave him a copy of the stats I'd been keeping for the tournament: fielding, batting, and pitching.

"The Falcons always look tough, don't they?" I said.

"Amazons," he said, and checked out the stats.

"They should be carrying axes instead of bats." I watched him study the stats. "As a team we're hitting .310 for the tournament," I pointed out. "Robinson has two home runs and five RBIs; she's hitting .347. Joy's pitched 9-⅓ innings and has given up three runs."

"Not so great," he said.

"But her last effort was a one-hitter. New Hampton scored two runs on an error," I reminded him. "She hasn't allowed an earned run in her last nine innings. Only four walks last game. That's great for her. Um . . . I have something else for you to look at."

"What?"

Handing him the second printout, I explained it carefully, telling him the same thing I'd told Joy. "These guys are fastball hitters. I knew that before, but these stats really make it clear."

"Where did you get this information?"

"I kept it in the computer."

"What's it prove?"

I looked at him, hoping my look didn't say I

thought he was stupid. "Joy needs to attack them with more curves, more off-speed stuff."

"That's not how to attack."

"Look what the Falcons have done to her fastball. It's the best, but they'll still hit it if that's all they see."

"You're not the coach here, Jeremy."

"Take their three, four, and five hitters—Monroe, Roemer, and Schroeder. Each one is hitting over .300 against Joy. Seventy percent of the team's hits have come on fastballs. Doesn't that tell you something?"

"Look, Jeremy, I keep telling you I appreciate what you do for the team, but I'll do the coaching. All right? I'll handle it." He thrust the printout back into my hand. "Keep it. Sit down and enjoy the game. We're going to be state champs."

"Not unless you listen to me."

His lips thinned. "Can it, Jeremy. You're a good kid, but you're not the coach." Turning and walking away, he headed for the water fountain by the Leafs' dugout.

I was mad, really mad. Couldn't he see beyond his nose? Couldn't he admit that someone might know more than he did?

As soon as the Leafs hustled out of the dugout to take infield, I yelled to Joy, calling her to the fence where I'd talked to Thorton a moment ago. "What?"

She wore her glove, pounding the pocket, getting ready to go.

"Did you bring the notebook?" I asked.

"Yes."

"Have you studied it?"

"Pretty much. Why?"

"Thorton barely looked at the information I gave him. He wouldn't listen to me. You're going to have to shake off his pitches and throw your own game. I'd start right away in the first inning. I wouldn't wait till I got into trouble."

"Kelley! Let's move it!" Thorton strode to the fence. "What the hell's going on, Jeremy?" Taking off his hat, he wiped the sweatband.

"We're planning on winning this game," I told him. I rolled up the batting report and stuck it in the chain-link fence. "That's your ticket to a state championship. It's free. You better take it."

His face turned red, and he slammed his hat back on his head. "You know what you can do with that—?"

Joy pulled the printout through the fence and held it out for Thorton. "I think Jeremy's right," she said. "This is my first and only chance. I've been playing since seventh grade for this." She looked him in the eye. "I don't want anybody to screw it up for me." Joy shoved the rolled up paper at him. He ignored it.

"I'm the coach here!" he snarled. "I'm the one who takes the blame if we lose."

"We're not going to lose," I said. "Not if you let Joy pitch her game."

"I'm not listening to two kids tell me how to run *my* team."

"*Your* team?" Joy's cheeks flushed.

"You don't *have* a team without Joy," I said.

Shoving the report at him again, Joy said, "That's right." Her eyes narrowed defiantly.

He looked at both of us. The way Joy thrust her chin out, I had no doubt she'd walk off the field if he didn't let her throw her pitches. I stared at him. I wondered if he was thinking of what kind of story old man Kelley might write for the morning paper if his daughter didn't pitch, especially if she explained why in the paper. And if the Leafs lost.

I said, "If Joy doesn't pitch, old man Kelley's going to make mincemeat out of you in the morning paper."

Thorton's jaw worked furiously, practically grinding his teeth to dust. Grabbing the report from Joy, he jammed it into his back pocket. "Get the hell on the field," he said to Joy. Then he growled at me: "I'm still the coach here. Remember that."

I looked at him, turned away, and left.

Chapter
28

THREE GIGGLING HIGH SCHOOL GIRLS WHO HAD BEEN pushing Darin around in his chair brought him back as the "National Anthem" stopped playing. One was a pretty, petite blond; the other two, brunettes. "Be ready to party tonight!" Darin told them.

"We will!" the girls sang. "See you later! Gotta go!"

Darin smelled of beer. "Minors contributing to your delinquency?" I asked.

"Couple of beers in the parking lot, that's all. You remember them, don't you? The Mau sisters and Lisa Deem, the blond."

"Vaguely."

"They know where there's a couple of parties to-night." Darin squinted at the scoreboard. "What's the score?"

"The national anthem just finished. How can there be a score?" I looked into Darin's eyes; they glittered like floodlights. "Man, what have you had to drink?"

"None of your business."

"Your dad doesn't want you drinking."

"None of his business, either."

"Right."

I turned to the game.

Over five thousand screaming, cheering fans had crowded into the ballpark. Excitement vibrated through the air, and my body tingled. I could hardly sit still. "Visitors" due to the toss of a coin, the Leafs had taken the field first. I couldn't wait for Joy to hum that first strike across the plate, to break off that first curve ball and catch the batter looking wide-eyed.

The Falcons' leadoff hitter stepped in, and my hands turned sweaty. Four fastballs and two curves—Joy struck her out to start the game.

"Way to go, Joy!" I screamed, jumping up.

"I hope she can keep it up," Darin said.

"She will!"

Joy walked the next Falcon on a 3–2 pitch. Though she had mixed in a tantalizing curve for a strike, the batter let it go. When the Falcons' number-three hitter, Jenny Roemer, came to the plate, she let two curves go by, then poked a whistling line drive—I held my breath—over the right-field fence. Foul! Another fastball. I let my breath out. I'd never been part of such a pressure-packed game. I wondered if I'd last.

Then I started thinking: although Joy had thrown five curves for strikes to the first three batters, no one had swung at one. I knew exactly what was happening. A crafty veteran, Falcon Coach Steve Saladino had apparently told his hitters to lay off the curve and wait for the fastball. Or the walk. Hell, Joy might get knocked off the mound in the first inning. I dropped my clipboards on the ground, stood, cupped my hand round my mouth, and boomed through the fence: "Joy! You got more than *two* pitches! Use them ALL!" I know she heard me. She didn't look my way, but I know she heard me. She shook off Thorton's next signal three times, then threw her drop for a second strike. Joy's next pitch, a curve on the inside corner, fooled Roemer again. She was out of there on a called third strike.

Yeah!

"I can't believe she's looking so good," Darin said.

"She's going to get even better." I was standing, clutching the fence, breathing hard.

"Hey, jerk! Do you have to keep jumping up in front of me?"

"Sorry." Settling back into my lawn chair, I arranged my charts on my knees, then watched the

Falcons' number-four hitter, Wanda Jackson, step into the batter's box with a runner on first. Around the conference Jackson was called "Wanda Whacker" because she had whacked sixteen home runs this season—three off Joy, one in the first inning of the first game we played against the Falcons. If Joy had studied the information I'd given her, she'd know that Wanda had hit those homers off fastballs.

Joy had done her homework.

Drop . . . drop . . . curve . . . drop—Wanda Whacker didn't see a fastball. Joy struck her out on four pitches, and I felt the biggest smile in the world spreading across my face.

"I can't believe it," Darin said.

"We're going to win this game," I told him.

The game was a delight to watch, a breathtaking masterpiece of pitching. Val Hightower was a six-two, solidly built pitcher with thighs and forearms like a man's; no doubt she did a lot of weight lifting. With her short brown hair and fierce scowl, Hightower looked like a prison warden. She had a fastball—not as good as Joy's—curve, and change-up. The change-up she often telegraphed. What made her a premier pitcher was her intimidating appearance and her pinpoint control; she threw for the corners and seldom missed.

Through three innings both pitchers were working on no-hitters. Hushed between pitches, the crowd roared at each strike, each ball, each hard grounder or line drive, each putout.

"This game is boring," Darin complained during the fourth inning. "Nothing's happening."

"Two pitchers are throwing no-hitters. How can you call that boring, man? In fact, Hightower's got a perfect game going—no hits, no walks, no errors."

"We need to kick ass," Darin said.

"We need a break."

In life, breaks often come from unexpected sources. Pee Wee Avila provided the Leafs with their break. Weighing maybe ninety-five pounds—uniform, spikes, batting helmet, and glove included—Pee Wee was a good leadoff singles hitter, with a great on-base percentage of .410 for the season.

In the top of the fifth with the Falcon outfield playing in and straight away, Hightower delivered a fastball down the pipe, and Pee Wee poked it high into the soft night air. Though I jumped up and held my breath, I thought surely the Falcon left-fielder, Rhonda Butler, would chase the ball down. But it seemed to develop wings; it sailed through the floodlights' glare in a high arch, then suddenly dropped straight down, bouncing off the pipe that runs along the top of the outfield's five-foot-high fence. Butler was only a step away from the fence, but the ball hit the pipe and bounded away from her, over the fence. A home run! No doubt about it.

I must've leapt six feet into the air. Our fans went out of their gourds. After Pee Wee wheeled around the bases and stomped on the plate, the Maple Leaf dugout rushed her, smothering her with hugs, kisses, slaps on the back.

"Did you see that?" I yelled at Darin. I was wild with happiness.

"I saw it. Now Joy needs to stay tough."

I collapsed in my lawn chair. For once Darin was right: Joy needed to continue handcuffing the Falcons. No runs. No hits. She'd walked one batter in each of the first four innings; that wasn't bad for her. An insurance run would be great. If the Leafs had a 2–0 advantage, the fat lady could start singing.

By the bottom of the sixth, Hightower was visibly frustrated: her team hadn't come close to scoring. She walked the Leafs' leadoff hitter, Shawna Lucas. Hightower hadn't walked a batter in forty innings—I'd read that stat in the paper this morning. Then she served up a long single to Corky. With no one out, Lucas pulled up at third, playing it safe.

My hopes for an insurance run soared. A hit, a good bunt, an error—if the Leafs simply put the ball in play, their insurance run was inevitable. But Hightower had a different idea. She showed what she was really made of: she struck out Barb Peters, Suzie Stiles, and Joy to end the inning. I felt deflated. Then I thought, *So what? The Leafs still lead 1–0. Joy has only one more inning to work.*

When Joy walked the Falcons' leadoff hitter, Val Hightower, on four pitches my stomach started to churn.

"We could be in trouble," I told Darin.

"She better not lose this thing," he said.

"She's probably nervous as hell. I know I am."

C'mon, babe. Settle down.

The Falcons' next hitter rapped an easy grounder to Corky. *Around the horn for a double play! Yeah!* But Corky's throw to second sailed high and wide of shortstop Suzie Stiles into center field. Before Bev could retrieve the ball and throw home, Hightower lumbered safely into third, the batter scooting to second. The error light flashed on the scoreboard.

Runners on second and third, nobody out—my nerves were live wires.

"This is it," Darin said.

I nodded. "This is it. If Joy doesn't get out of this, we're dead." I couldn't imagine what it must be like standing on that mound, knowing the game was on your shoulders. I think I would have caved in.

On Joy's next pitch, I leapt to my feet again.

"Sit down!" Darin yelled.

The batter squared around to bunt, and Hightower broke for the plate. Joy snapped off a beautiful curve; the batter missed the ball. And so did Shawna. The pitch kicked off her glove and bounded to the backstop. Hightower broke for home. If her coach told her to go, he hadn't counted on Joy's quickness. She streaked to the plate, took Shawna's underhand toss, and whirled to put the tag on Hightower, only two feet away.

The collision was spectacular. Neither girl had time to think about what was going to happen; it just happened. Hightower lowered her shoulder and caught Joy under the chin, knocking Joy flat on her back, planting her, Joy's head hitting the ground and bouncing, as Hightower fell on her.

Crunch!

The umpire cried, "You're out!"

Shawna immediately yelled for a time-out.

"What's happening?" Darin said. "Sit down!"

Hightower jumped up to argue with the umpire.

Suddenly I wasn't watching Hightower. I was watching Joy, my heart stopping. Joy lay on her back, writhing on the ground. Then I couldn't see her as Thorton and the infield came charging to her, surrounding her.

"Ox!" I screamed at Hightower as she trotted to her dugout.

I bit my lip. I shouldn't have yelled that. The collision wasn't her fault—it was clean, hard-nosed softball—but I was out of my mind. I don't know what kept me from climbing the fence and running onto the field to help Joy.

Then through a tiny break in the crowd of people

surrounding Joy, I glimpsed her coughing or gagging or something as people lifted her to her feet. Then it looked as if she wobbled and collapsed on the ground again. I couldn't tell.

"Get a stretcher!" I screamed. "Get her out of there. SHE'S PREGNANT! You've got to get her out of there! You hear me? SHE'S PREGNANT!"

"What?" Darin's voice seemed far away.

I whirled. I didn't know what I was saying. "She's PREGNANT I'm telling you. They've got to get her out of there! She's—" My mouth was open, my voice stuck in my throat.

"What did you say?" Darin spoke through gritted teeth, his eyes hot and dark in his pale face.

A cold chill swept through me. "Darin, listen to me. I swear I don't know what I was saying. I swear—"

"You said Joy was pregnant!"

I breathed deeply. "Darin, you have to listen— You have to believe me—" Applause and a roar erupted from the crowd. I glanced at the field. The Maple Leaf players had gone back to their positions. Joy was on her feet, hanging on to Thorton and the Leafs' trainer. Each guy held one of her arms, and they were helping her to the dugout.

"They shouldn't put Joy back in—"

"Because she's pregnant?" Lightning bolts of hate flashed in his eyes.

I was so confused I didn't know what to do. The game was important, but—

And then Darin went crazy. Right there in front of my eyes with rows and rows of spectators behind us, he started flailing his arms, throwing his head about, and screaming all the obscenities in the world. I knew people were staring at him, pointing. I thought police or security guards might come after us; they'd be able to tell he'd been drinking. I had no choice: I had to get him out of there.

Chapter
29

AFTER DRAWING THE STRAP ON DARIN'S CHAIR ACROSS his waist to hold him in and buckling it in back—he might have flung himself onto the ground—I wrapped my arms around his chest, holding his arms down, and pushed him out of the park. I couldn't keep his mouth shut, though; he kept screaming obscenities. Twisting their necks, the few people walking by who were not in the stands watching the game looked at Darin, then at me as if I were pushing a crazy person. Maybe I was.

One guy stopped and said, "Need help, buddy?"

"Naw. He'll be OK."

After I had wheeled Darin into the parking lot, that's when I did it. I slapped him. Not hard. Just hard enough to get his attention.

The slap shut him up instantly. On the gravel lot, surrounded by tall poles topped with floodlights, I dropped to one knee by his chair, steadying him with my hands on his shoulders.

"Darin, I'm sorry." I shook him a little. "Darin, I had to." He wasn't looking at me. He was staring past my face into the distance at the rows of parked cars, his eyes burning dark and bright, sunken in his head, his face dead-white.

I looked back at the stadium a hundred yards away. Was Joy OK? Was she hurt badly, or had she gone back to the mound? The Falcon coach wouldn't let Thorton stall the game for more than a minute or two because of an injury to Joy. Annie Meyer could be on the mound, getting blasted. Suddenly I heard a roar erupt from the park. I had no way of knowing what happened. Maybe Joy was back in the game, and somebody tagged her for a home run. Or had she struck the next batter out? With the breeze coming from the wrong direction, the sound from the P.A. wouldn't carry that far.

I turned back to Darin. His face was stone; he wasn't blinking. "Darin, are you all right?"

No answer.

"Darin, I'm taking you home."

As I headed the van through the night, I wanted desperately to turn on the radio and catch the game summary. The game could be over, the championship decided, unless the Falcon runner on third tied the score 1–1, sending the game into extra innings. How was Joy? What about the baby? Who was on the mound? I'd pushed Darin out of the park so fast, I'd forgotten my lawn chair, score book, and pitching chart.

I didn't turn the radio on, though; I kept talking to Darin and glancing back at him in the rearview mirror, telling him I was his friend. I might have betrayed him, but I was still his friend. My heart wrenched as I kept glancing at him. He was rocking back and forth from the waist up, like autistic kids do, sort of in a trance. I kept talking to him, reminding him of the fun things we did as kids. "Hey, Darin, remember . . ."

"Screw you!" he hissed.

I glanced in the mirror again. At least he could talk.

When I turned the van into the drive at Darin's house, I decided I couldn't dump him off, then leave. I had to explain to his folks what had happened. They needed to watch him so he didn't do something stupid. And somehow I had to warn Joy about what had happened. Win or lose, she'd be arriving soon to pick up Darin for a round of partying. I couldn't let her rush into this situation cold.

As I lowered Darin out of the van and wheeled him up the ramp to the front porch, he didn't say a word. Mrs. Steele, dressed in yellow shorts and halter, opened the door for us, smiling. "I've been listening. The game's over. We won!"

Scared as I was, I felt my face light up. "The score?"

"One—nothing. Weren't you at the game? How did you get here so soon?"

"We left early," I said.

Mrs. Steele looked immediately at Darin. "Sweetheart, are you all right?"

He didn't answer.

"Jeremy, he looks as if he's seen a ghost. What's wrong?"

"Um . . ." I cleared my throat. "Where's Mr. Steele?" I didn't want to explain to Mrs. Steele. I thought I'd have better luck talking to her husband.

"At a meeting. Why are you home so early?" Mrs. Steele reached for Darin's hand. "Sweetheart, what's wrong? Joy won. Aren't you happy? She'll surely get an Iowa scholarship."

Jerking his hand away, Darin snarled, "Leave me alone! Both of you!" Mrs. Steele looked at him calmly, undisturbed. She'd seen him like this before—everyone had.

"Has he been drinking?" Mrs. Steele asked.

"He said some girls gave him a couple of beers. I don't know what else."

"So that's it," she said.

I shifted my weight from one foot to the other. "Mrs. Steele, could I talk to you alone?"

A smile flickered across her face. "Certainly, Jeremy. What is it?"

"It would be easier if . . . you know, if we could be alone a moment."

I cast another look at Darin; his face was tight and sullen. I wished I could read his mind. Was he planning something bizarre?

"Darin, sweetheart, would you like to watch TV?"

Darin didn't answer.

Mrs. Steele pushed him in front of the wide-screen TV in the living room and turned on late local news for him. "They might mention the game on TV. Joy pitched a no-hitter."

She stuck the remote control in Darin's hand, and he stared at the screen as it flashed from commercial to commercial.

"He'll be all right for a moment," Mrs. Steele said. She motioned me to follow her down a long hall to her bedroom. Though the Steeles' air-conditioned house always chilled me, I began to feel warm, and my knees were turning to jelly.

Snapping on a light, she closed the door when I entered. The room filled with rose-colored light from two lamps on her dressing table, and the scent of her perfume hung heavily in the air. Sitting on a queen-sized water bed, she crossed her legs and patted a place next to her.

"All right, Jeremy. Come sit next to me. Tell me what this is all about."

I tugged at the collar of my T-shirt. "I'll stand, thank you. This has to be quick."

Mrs. Steele smiled.

"I mean, uh, we can't leave Darin alone very long. He might do something stupid to himself."

"Why do you say that?" She patted the bed again. "I'm not going to bite."

I held my breath a second, then exhaled. "Mrs. Steele, Joy's pregnant."

Surprise flashed in her eyes, then delight, and then her face broke into a grin. "I never expected. I mean, I prayed that Darin and Joy would some-day—" She stopped, her eyes suddenly narrowing suspiciously. "Why are you telling me this? Why isn't Darin telling me?"

My hands clutched. "Because I'm responsible. I'm the one who's made Joy pregnant." My hands clutched again. "And tonight Darin found out. That's why he's upset."

"You *told* him?"

I shook my head. "He found out by accident." I explained what happened. "I was going to tell him anyway," I said, "but not for a couple of days." Tears stung my eyes.

Don't cry in front of her, Jeremy.

"You are a bastard!" Mrs. Steele's face turned scarlet. "A real bastard, Jeremy Logan." She stood, the muscles in her neck tightening. "How could you? You, his best friend. You bastard!"

"I never intended to hurt Darin."

"I asked you once if you were lonely. Remember that night on the front steps? I told you I was here for you. I made everything quite obvious. I told you what it's like living with a man who the moment he comes home drinks till he falls into bed. What more could I say to you?"

"He goes to AA now."

Mrs. Steele dismissed the thought with an angry wave of her hand. "Why do you think I made myself available?"

"Mrs. Steele—"

"I could see this happening. I knew you liked Joy. I could see it in your eyes, the way you looked at her. The way she looked at you. Darin could tell."

"Mrs. Steele, I never wanted this to happen."

"I thought we might both do ourselves some good, you and me. If it's fun you wanted—"

"Mrs. Steele, listen to me!" I was shouting. "*I didn't want you!*"

Mrs. Steele stared at me a moment; her laugh was quick and scornful. "Joy hasn't told you, has she?"

"Told me what?"

Mrs. Steele threw her head back, laughing again, mocking me, just as Darin liked to do. "She may have your baby, but she'll always belong to Darin."

Turning abruptly, Mrs. Steele strode to her dressing table, bent and looked at herself in the mirror, fluffing her hair, her hoop earrings glittering. "Leave, Jeremy."

"Joy loves *me*, not Darin."

Mrs. Steele whirled from the dressing table, clutching a hairbrush. "I want you out of this house. Immediately!"

"I have to be here when Joy talks to Darin. I have to make it clear to him this was all my fault."

"Darin will be happy to hear that. I'll tell him. Leave—"

"Mrs. Steele—"

"—or I'll call the police." The muscles in her neck were quivering. "And if you ever come back, I'll call them. Good-bye, Jeremy."

Chapter
30

I PARKED SIX BLOCKS FROM DARIN'S HOUSE, ON HIS street, and waited in the darkness of my car. It was eleven o'clock, the night cool, the stars and moon bright. No tree in the Sunnyside subdivision was big enough to block them out. From where I sat, I could see a string of car lights flickering two miles away on the highway: Maple Grove fans returning from Riverbend, savoring victory, getting ready to party. The faint but jubilant sound of car horns spread the word: Maple Grove was state champ.

I waited for Joy. I knew she'd be headed for Darin's. Regardless of what Mrs. Steele had said, I wasn't going to let her go into that house alone to deal with Darin. If Mrs. Steele wouldn't let me in, I wouldn't let Joy in. The answer to that problem was simple.

A tougher question pounded in my brain: what was the terrible power Darin held over Joy?

Joy hasn't told you, has she? I heard Mrs. Steele's words again.

What was the stranglehold? There had to be more to the answer than her being his girlfriend once, his being in a wheelchair.

At eleven-fifteen, I spotted headlights in the Buick's rearview mirror; they cut through the night, racing up behind me. The driver had to be Joy. I waited till the car sailed by—red Escort—and I followed. When Joy stopped at the stop sign two blocks from Darin's, I pulled alongside her and shouted through my open window that it was me; she should pull over.

Surprise lighted her face. Rolling down her window, she said, "What?"

"Pull over. I need to talk to you."

She crossed the intersection and parked. I pulled in front of her, shut the Buick down, and got out. When I opened the Escort's door and slid in beside her, Joy was frowning. "Where were you and Darin after the game? I looked all over for you guys. Some fan found your score book and pitching chart and gave them to Thorton. Where were you guys? Did you see what happened?"

"You won on a no-hitter, right?"

"Oh, God, Jeremy, I'm so glad I listened to you."

She was breathless with excitement, her words tumbling from her lips. "I felt good on the mound, and every pitch made me feel better. Even when I walked someone, I knew I had the stuff to get the next batter out." She shivered with delight. "This is so neat! We're state champs!" Flinging her arms round my neck, she hugged me and kissed me on the cheek. Then she bubbled with more questions: "Where's Darin? How long have you been following me? How did you lose your score book and pitching chart?"

I took her hands and squeezed them. "Joy, listen to me. A lot of things have happened tonight."

Victory had wound Joy too tight to listen. "Wasn't it awesome?" she bubbled. "Sixteen tournament teams parading onto the field for the presentations, did you see that? We all got roses. Look, there's mine"—she pointed at the dashboard—"and the medal is beautiful. Look in the glove compartment. You should see how big the first-place trophy really is when you have to hold it. I'm captain of the all-tournament team, Jeremy! Two scouts talked to me after the game. One was from Iowa. One was from Oklahoma and said he'd never seen a better-pitched high school game. . . ." Joy threw her arms around me again and this time kissed me on the mouth.

I didn't think she was ever going to stop talking. I sat listening, happy for Joy but frightened of what I had to tell her.

"Why are we sitting here?" she asked, finally winding down. "Darin's going to be worried." She stopped. "Is something wrong?"

I closed my eyes a second. "You know when Hightower knocked you down?"

"Was that a collision, or what? But I held onto the ball."

"I thought you'd really gotten hurt."

"She knocked the wind out of me."

"I couldn't see very well, all those people standing around you. At one point, I thought you were on the ground on your hands and knees gagging. When you got to your feet, you looked wobbly."

"I wasn't gagging. I was coughing up a little dust. I went back to the dugout for a second and got a drink of water. I came back out ready to go, a little sore, but that was all."

"I thought you were hurt. I mean, really hurt bad. Hightower flattened you."

"She did *not*. She knocked me down. Not flattened." Sitting back against her door, her elbow on the steering wheel, Joy asked, "What are you getting at, Jeremy?"

"After you went down, I started yelling at Hightower and at Thorton. I didn't know I was saying it, I swear."

"What were you saying?"

"I didn't know. That's the truth. I heard my words

seconds later, like I was hearing my voice played back on a tape recorder."

"*What*, Jeremy?"

I bit my lower lip. "I was yelling something like, 'She's pregnant. You've got to get her out of there! She's pregnant.' "

"You said *that?*"

"And Darin heard me."

"Oh, God." Joy stared through the windshield.

"I didn't mean to tell him. Not that way. It was an accident."

Her hands were fists in her lap.

I moved closer to her. "I'd never do anything to ruin this night for you, whether the Leafs won or lost. You have to believe that." She didn't say anything. "Joy?" She wouldn't look at me.

In the dim light, I watched as she began slowly twisting Darin's friendship ring around and around on her finger. "What did Darin say?"

"He lost it," I said. "He started flailing his arms and cussing so bad people started staring at him and pointing. I wheeled him out of the park. I didn't see the end of the game. He was all I could manage. That's how I left the score book and chart behind. Even in the parking lot I couldn't get him quiet. Till I slapped him."

"You slapped him?"

"He wouldn't shut up. Then he went into one of

his moods, where he isolates himself and stares into space. I took him home like that. I tried to explain to his mother."

Joy was shaking her head.

"I would have rather talked to Mr. Steele," I said, "but he was at an AA meeting. I told her you were pregnant, I was responsible, Darin knew, and I was afraid he might do something to himself. Mrs. Steele threw me out of the house."

"Do you think he *will* do something?"

I shrugged. "I don't know. Mrs. Steele didn't seem worried. She was more concerned about your still belonging to Darin. She said you'd always belong to him." I hesitated. "Is that true?"

Joy didn't answer, only stared out the windshield, so I launched another question: "Did you and Darin ever . . . you know, what you said?"

Joy lowered her head, twisting Darin's ring again. "No, we haven't done it. Twice when we were together this week . . . I thought about it, but I couldn't." Joy slid Darin's ring off her finger, then slid it back on. "He's not the same. He's not the Darin I knew. The chair has changed him. I mean, his mind, the way he is inside—Darin's not there anymore. I couldn't . . . The lie I was going to tell him is worse than the truth." Joy wiped the corners of her eyes with her fingertips. "Let's go talk to him," she said.

"You mean it?"

"Yes."

I said, "I'm going to tell him I never meant to hurt him or steal you. I want to be his friend, if he'll let me. I want him to forgive us. That . . . that I can't help it: I love you."

Joy started the Escort, and it purred to life. I opened my door to get out to drive my Buick.

She turned on her headlights. In the dim dash lights, her face looked pale but soft and loving. "I'm going to tell him the same thing," she said. "And that I love you."

Chapter
31

HOLDING HANDS, JOY AND I STOOD ON DARIN'S FRONT porch. I rang the doorbell, listening to the four-note chime. Lights lit the house, but the backyard was dark, so I figured nobody was poolside. Crickets chirped.

Joy's hand was sweaty, and she was trembling. "Hey, take it easy. This won't be as bad as you think." I squeezed her hand. "Darin already knows. It's not like we have to break the news to him"—I shuffled my feet—"though Mrs. Steele said if I came to her house again she was going to call the cops."

"It'll be worse than you think," Joy said.

At that moment the porch light flicked on and the door opened. Mrs. Steele stood before us, her chin thrust forward. "I told you never to come back." She looked right at me.

"We want to talk to Darin." Suddenly my throat was dry.

"It's really necessary, Mrs. Steele." Joy's voice shook. I squeezed her hand again.

"I shouldn't let either of you in this house." The ice in Mrs. Steele's words chilled the warm night. "But Darin wants to see both of you."

"Is he all right?" Joy said.

"All right?" Mrs. Steele glared at Joy. "How could he be all right? Not after what you've done to him." Mrs. Steele shook a finger at Joy. "We had an agreement, you and I."

"Agreement?" I said.

"Tell him," Mrs. Steele said. "Tell him so he knows and gets out of your life."

I pulled the screen door open.

Joy and I stepped into the house.

"Darin's by the pool," Mrs. Steele said, "sitting in the dark. He won't come in. I'm afraid to leave him there and go to bed. Howard's not home yet. Darin can't make sense out of what both of you have done to him."

Leading Joy by the hand, I walked through the house and slid the glass door to the patio open. Darin sat in the darkness, looking at the pool.

"You want lights?" I asked.

"No lights." His voice was dry, brittle.

"Hi," Joy said softly.

I suddenly felt sorry for Darin. I knew what it

was like to sit in the dark, turning your thoughts over and over in your mind, feeling betrayed.

Each pulling up a patio chair, Joy and I sat close to Darin. He was staring at the pool water. With only the moon and stars for light, I couldn't make out the expression in his eyes or on his face, only that his jawline was rigid.

"We won," Joy said. "We're state champs." She touched his hand. "There's some serious partying to do tonight."

Darin drew his hand away. "You *bitch!*"

I said, "Darin, let's all be cool, OK?"

"You stay out of it! This is between me and Joy. I want you around only to hear a couple of things."

"Darin, *please* listen to us," Joy said.

"We came here to explain," I said. "And to apologize. . . ."

"And to tell the truth," Joy said.

"The truth?" Darin said. "The honest-to-God *truth?* Have you told *him* the truth, Joy?"

"Darin, please . . ."

"I want you to tell him now." Darin looked up at Joy, his long black hair framing his slender face. "I want him to hear it."

"You don't have to tell me anything, Joy."

"Tell him, Joy. I want to make sure you tell it right. Tell it now."

Joy closed her eyes a moment and nodded her

head slowly. "Jeremy, you have to listen to this."

"You don't have to tell me anything," I repeated.

"Oh, yes she does, man. Shut up and listen."

Joy slipped Darin's ring off her finger and held it in the palm of her hand, staring at it as she spoke: "The night of Darin's injury we were going to make love," she said. "It was midnight. His parents were in bed. It was dark like this by the pool, just the stars and moon out."

"Skip the stars and moon," Darin said. "Tell him how we were making out."

"Shut up, Darin," I said. "Joy, you don't have to say another word."

"It's all right. I want to tell it." Joy pushed on, each word she spoke piercing me. "We were going to do it for the first time," she said. "I was teasing Darin. I made him chase me. I said we'd do it if he could catch me. He was pretty drunk. I kept running around the pool. I'll wear him out, I thought. I didn't realize how determined he was. He must have chased me round the pool ten minutes. He wouldn't give up, but I knew he'd never catch me.

"I was hot and sweaty. I don't know exactly why I said it—I guess I was ready to give in—and I yelled, 'Catch me in the pool!' I jumped from the side of the pool into the deep part. Darin forgot what end he was at. He dove into the shallow part. . . ."

"And that," Darin said, "is all I remember, man.

One moment I was going for it, the next I was doomed to a wheelchair. I hate it when that happens."

I looked at Darin in his chair, his body rocking, his hands working. No matter how I felt about him, I realized fate had dealt him a horrible blow.

"Why aren't you laughing, man? Don't you think it's funny? I think it's hilarious. I go for it for the first time and I end up paralyzed. That didn't happen to you, did it, Jeremy?"

I couldn't answer.

"It happened to me."

Joy let out a little breath of air and squared her shoulders. "I got Darin off the bottom and his face out of the water," she said. "He was unconscious, and he was too heavy; I couldn't drag him out of the pool. I yelled and yelled for his parents. His mom finally heard me and came running out to the pool, where she found us, me still holding Darin's head out of the water. I was hysterical and couldn't explain very well what happened, but Mrs. Steele figured out most of the details herself."

"What's there to figure?" Darin asked. "Joy Kelley put me in this chair. The truth is as simple as that."

"You put yourself there," I said. "Joy didn't force that beer down your throat."

"I put him there. I made him chase me." Joy was staring again at Darin's ring in her palm.

"Don't you think she owes me a little something for a broken neck, Jeremy?"

"She owes you nothing! You got yourself drunk!"

"You know what she made me promise? That I'd never tell anyone how this really happened—that we were running around the pool naked. She didn't want anyone—especially you, Jeremy—to know what a naughty little girl she is. My mother promised not to tell her parents." Darin leaned toward Joy and shook a finger in her face. "But you didn't keep your part of the deal, did you?"

"What deal?" I asked.

Darin laughed. "You *are* stupid," he said. "She always liked you better, but you had to wait till I was in a chair to find the courage to do anything about it, didn't you? Well, that's tough, buddy, because she's still mine. She'll get rid of your kid and still be mine. God, that's funny."

I grabbed Joy's hand. "I have to get out of here before I kill him. Let's go." Joy was starting to cry. I stood and pulled her up from the chair. "Hey, it's all right. Don't cry. The truth's out; it can't hurt anyone anymore. You're free, and we don't have to lie. Everything's cool. Let's go."

"You can leave by yourself, Jeremy," Darin said. "That's all I wanted you for—to hear the truth."

Joy turned to Darin. "I'm not getting an abortion."

"My family will pay for it. My mother told me that tonight."

"I don't care," Joy said.

"Fine," he said. "Have the baby adopted."

Hairs bristled on my neck. "No way!"

"Back off!" Darin flared. "Don't you understand? She owes me! She knows that. She's known since the moment she knew my neck was broken that she'd have to pay the price for the rest of her life—"

"No, she doesn't!"

"—just like me."

"The mistake was yours! *You* drank the beer!" I grabbed him by the shirt, twisting. "If you love her, let her *go!* Or I'll—!" I raised my hand to hit him.

"Jeremy, don't!"

"Go ahead! Hit me again!" he snarled in my face.

"Jeremy!" Joy grabbed my arm and hung on.

"I'm trapped. She's trapped. That's the way it is, man. Hit me! It won't change anything."

"Jeremy, please!"

Joy wrenched at my arm, and I lowered it, but I kept twisting Darin's shirt, making a knot of it under his chin. "You're the stupid one!" I said.

"Jeremy, let him go! You're choking him!"

My chest was bursting, and I could hardly breathe. "If you really loved her, you'd let her *go!*" I said between clenched teeth, twisting his shirt once more, then suddenly releasing it. A few more twists of his shirt and I might have killed him. What kind of maniac chokes a guy in a wheelchair? My knees felt so weak I could hardly stand.

Darin gasped and felt his throat.

"Are you all right?" Joy knelt and stroked Darin's forehead. "Are you all right?"

"I'm all right." He gulped. "But that bastard's crazy."

I turned away from them, sick at the sight of them together, disgusted with myself, at what I'd nearly done. My chest still heaved.

"Are you sure you're all right?" Joy asked again.

"I'm fine," Darin said, and laughed mockingly. "A couple of years ago I would've killed him for laying a hand on me or you. I still will someday."

A silence followed as I blinked at the sky and stars, unable to hold off tears of anger and frustration. Nothing was working out the way I wanted it to.

Then Darin asked, "What are you doing?"

"This is yours," I heard Joy answer quietly.

I turned.

Joy took Darin's hand, opened it, and pressed the ring into his palm. "It doesn't belong to me." She folded his fingers over the ring. "I don't belong to you. You'll have to get strong by yourself. You can do it. You'll walk again someday, but I can't be your crutch any longer. You have to do it on your own. You'll be stronger if you do it on your own. And you can't feel sorry for yourself anymore, even if what happened wasn't your fault. You were a victim." Joy was crying. "You'll be better off without me. I'm so sorry I hurt you."

Darin was too stunned to even look up. I was as stunned as Darin. He stared at the ring in his palm, and I stood motionless.

"Good-bye, Darin." Joy kissed him on the forehead. "Let's go," she said to me, tears sliding down her cheeks. Then to Darin, "We'll tell your mother we're leaving."

I grabbed Joy's hand.

"You owe me!" Darin cried. "You owe me! *Both* of you!" he kept screaming. "*Both* of you!"

When Joy and I got to the sliding patio door, Darin had stopped yelling. I glanced back and froze.

I glimpsed Darin propelling himself across the patio in his chair. My mouth open to cry "Stop!" I stood dumb, my heart slamming against my ribcage, as he tumbled himself headlong into the deep end of the swimming pool with a splash.

Chapter
32

JOY WAS REACHING TO SLIDE THE PATIO DOORS OPEN, so she didn't see Darin aim his chair across the patio, but she heard the splash, saw the spray.

"It's Darin!" I screamed. "He wheeled himself into the pool!"

"Oh, no!"

I streaked for the pool and dove into the warm water, Joy a step behind me. The chair had carried Darin straight to the bottom: ten feet of water. He landed with his forehead on the pool bottom, the chair wheels pointed up. Joy and I uprighted the chair with Darin in it. His head bobbing, his arms limp, Darin made no effort to fight us. Each grabbing a shoulder, Joy and I struggled to lift him out of the chair but couldn't; the damned chair wanted to come with him. I'd been underwater only a half-minute but already felt as if my lungs were bursting and I heard my blood pounding in my ears. Then I remembered: at the ballpark, I'd strapped Darin into the chair to keep him from flailing. I felt for the buckle behind the chair, found and unsnapped it. Joy clamped her arm around his torso, kicking for the surface, Darin in her grasp. I broke the surface after them, gasping, ready to explode.

Towing Darin, Joy swam him to the side of the pool. "I'll help get him out," I yelled. I climbed out first, then hung onto him at the pool's edge while Joy climbed out. His eyes were closed, and his forehead oozed blood. He'd skinned it on the pool bottom. We both lifted him carefully out of the water and onto the deck.

The patio and pool lights popped on, and suddenly Mrs. Steele was at our sides, freaking out. She must have heard the commotion, or maybe she was watching and listening to what we'd been saying. I don't know.

"He's dead!" she was screaming. "He's dead! You killed him!"

I went berserk. "He's not *dead!*" I yelled. My ear was on his chest, listening to his heart thumping.

Had he broken his neck again? Was all the progress he'd made recently wasted? Would he be a quadriplegic again? Forever?

"Call an ambulance," I told Mrs. Steele.

"Call 911," Joy said.

"You killed him!" Mrs. Steele was shrieking again and again, her face contorted like a mad woman's.

"I'll call!" I said, and raced to the house.

When I came back, I brought a quilt from the couch in the den to wrap around Darin. Joy was supporting Darin's head, and he was vomiting water, his eyes bobbing around in their sockets.

"He's going to be all right," Joy said.

"I hope so," I said, laying the blanket over him.

An ambulance arrived, red lights flashing, sirens wailing. Ambulance attendants scooped Darin onto a stretcher and hauled him around the house to the front. Mrs. Steele leapt into the back of the ambulance, the back doors banging closed. Lights flicked on in the neighbors' houses, and people stood in their pajamas and robes on their front porches and on the sidewalk to see what was happening. Joy was crying in my arms, hot tears running down her cheeks.

"It's not our fault," I kept telling her. "It's not our fault."

"Yes, it is," she sobbed.

Chapter 33

AFTER THE AMBULANCE ZIPPED AWAY WITH DARIN AND his mother in it, Joy scribbled a note for Mr. Steele. Leaving it on the bar in the rec room, she explained that Darin had had an accident. An ambulance had taken him to Mercy Hospital in Riverbend. Mrs. Steele was with him.

Joy and I drove to the hospital and arrived shortly after the ambulance. Darin had already been admitted. A nurse told us they were moving him from emergency to intensive care, as a precaution. We begged for information about his condition.

"He seems to be resting nicely," the nurse said, looking at us suspiciously.

We were still wet from our dive into the pool, and our Nikes squished when we walked. I wondered if she recognized us as the hated enemy: winners over

Riverbend in the state softball tournament. We both wore Maple Grove colors: green shorts, white T-shirts.

"Is he going to be all right?" I asked.

"You can call in the morning for a condition report, but I think he's fine."

"Can we see him?" Joy smoothed her wet hair back. "Please?"

"His mother left word that he was to have no visitors."

"We're his best friends," I said. The words just came out. Joy and I exchanged a sheepish glance.

"I'm sorry," the nurse said. "You can't see him."

"That's not fair!" Joy said.

The nurse turned away.

Joy was going after her, but I grabbed Joy's hand. "There's nothing we can do. Come on."

"It's not fair."

Not knowing what else to do, we decided to wait in the lobby on the chance that Mrs. Steele would come by and at least tell us how Darin was. Suddenly Mr. Steele came rushing through the lobby's sliding glass doors. He was breathless, a desperate look in his eyes.

"I saw the ambulance on the highway," he said, and tried to catch his breath. "I had an eerie feeling it was Darin. Then I read your note. What happened? You're wet. Is Darin all right?"

"We think he's all right," Joy said.

"What happened?"

I looked at Joy. She looked at me. I went for the truth. No more lies. "Mr. Steele," I said, "Joy and I love each other. Joy's pregnant, and Darin found out tonight. He wheeled himself into the deep end of your swimming pool. Joy and I pulled him out." That was as brief and honest as I could make the story. I held my breath and waited for Mr. Steele's reaction.

He nodded slowly. "I knew you were in love. Everyone could tell. You can't hide love. What floor's Darin on?"

Joy and I shook our heads. "We don't know," Joy said. "Mrs. Steele left orders that we couldn't see him."

Mr. Steele checked at the nurses' station. Then he told us to follow him. We rode the elevator to the fourth floor. As we scurried down the hallway, many room doors gaped open. Inside, patients groaned; tiny white, yellow, and red machine lights blinked. The hallway smelled of antiseptics. A nurse glided by us, carrying a tiny tray with a paper cup of medicine.

"Wait in the waiting room," Mr. Steele said. "I'll find out about Darin."

Joy and I waited in the same room where we had waited for Darin twenty-four months ago. We sat in chairs in the dimly lit room. Magazines still littered the tables. Smelly cigarette butts and ashes filled the ashtrays. I moved the one on the table next to me to a table across the room. Pictures of mountains, a sailing ship at sea, and a lake hung crookedly on the walls.

I slumped into a chair next to Joy and held her hand. "Mr. Steele should put a lid on his wife's swimming pool," I said.

Joy gave me a frown.

"Sorry. I was just . . . trying to lighten things up."

"Do you think Darin will ever forgive us?" Joy asked.

"Maybe some things can never be forgiven. 'Sorry' isn't good enough."

Mr. and Mrs. Steele came into the room, Mr. Steele guiding his wife by her elbow. When she saw Joy and me, her face froze into an angry, hard look. Without makeup and with her lips turned down grimly, she looked old. "What are you doing here? I told you you couldn't see Darin."

"I met them in the lobby," Mr. Steele said. "I told them to come along and wait."

"I don't want them near Darin." She swept her hand through her hair. "You don't know what they've done to him."

"I know exactly what they've done." Mr. Steele looked at Joy and me with his gray eyes. "Darin's going to be all right. They've given him something to make sure he sleeps the night. There's no point in your hanging around. Mrs. Steele and I are going to wait a little longer. Just to make sure he's resting comfortably."

"You don't have to come back," Mrs. Steele said. "I don't want either of you to see Darin again."

"You can visit Darin whenever you please," Mr. Steele said. "You can come over to the house to see him."

Mrs. Steele's eyes flashed. "Howard! These kids tried a second time to kill Darin."

Joy gasped, and we both stood.

"That's a lie!" I cried. "*You're* killing him!"

"They've been sleeping together. Joy's pregnant."

"Enough!" Mr. Steele said, his voice rising.

A heavyset nurse came to the door and poked her head in. "What's going on?" She gave us an ugly scowl.

I wanted to hide.

"Is something wrong?" the nurse asked.

Mr. Steele collected himself and cleared his throat. "Nothing's wrong. We're . . . sorry for the noise."

The nurse scowled at us another moment. "There are sick people in this hospital. Please keep your voices down."

"Yes . . . we will," Mr. Steele said. "We will."

When the nurse turned and stalked away, shaking her head, Mr. and Mrs. Steele turned on each other.

"Margaret, listen to me," Mr. Steele said.

Mrs. Steele hissed, "I don't want these two to see Darin again."

"These kids are in love," Mr. Steele said. "They did what they had to do. They told Darin. They've put themselves and Darin on a very difficult road. But they can survive. We can all survive."

Mrs. Steele leveled her eyes on Joy and me. "Darin trusted both of them," she said bitterly. "What did it get him?" Suddenly huge tears formed in her eyes.

Mr. Steele nodded. "Besides learning to walk again, Darin has something else to learn: loving means looking beyond one's self to the needs of others." Mr. Steele circled his arm around his wife's shoulders and kissed her on the forehead. "I failed Darin before. Maybe I can do better this time," he said.

Mrs. Steele's face crumbled, and she began to cry as she covered her face with her hands.

I didn't know what to say. I had never seen Mrs. Steele fall apart, had never seen her vulnerable. I looked at Joy. Tears had gathered in her eyes, too. My feet began to shift.

Mr. Steele sensed how uncomfortable Joy and I were.

"Look," he said, "give Darin some time. Call in a week or two. Maybe it'll take longer, I don't know—a year. But keep calling. Stay in contact. You can always talk to me. I think we'll eventually find the old Darin, even if he is in a wheelchair. Be in touch."

"All right," Joy said, and tried to smile.

"We will," I added.

Mr. Steele squeezed his wife's shoulders.

Lowering her hands from her tear-stained face, Mrs. Steele looked at Joy and me again. Blankly, this time. Squaring her shoulders, she gathered her strength. "Good night," she said evenly.

"Good night," Joy and I replied.

We left after that. We didn't know what to do next. We needed a place where we could be alone, a place where we could pause a moment to sort out what had happened. Maple Grove had won the state tournament, Darin knew the truth, and he had attempted suicide. But there was hope for him. Mrs. Steele had crumbled. Mr. Steele was in charge. The night had been unreal.

What would happen to Joy and me?

Chapter
34

I PARKED IN THE CEMETERY IN OUR FAVORITE SPOT: the spot where I had parked Darin's van when he and Joy had invited me to the prom in April, where Joy and I had parked when we made love the first time. Tonight the moon and stars were shining brightly, crickets chirping, tombstones and pines standing guard.

After I shut the Buick down in the cemetery and turned out the lights, moonlit darkness enveloped us. I turned to Joy. She let out a little groan and suddenly leaned against me.

"Oh, Jeremy . . ."

We flung our arms around each other and hugged as hard as we could for a long time. Just hugged. Every once in a while Joy shivered.

The thought of leaving Joy pained me, twisting my stomach into knots. She was the first and the only girl I'd loved. I'd won her love, and in a few weeks I'd have to leave her. Once I had looked forward to being in the navy; suddenly I hated the idea. I wanted my arms around Joy always.

How could I be in love and feel so miserable? Be so scared?

"Your mother was right," I said when we finally let go of each other. "Darin had a stranglehold on you, didn't he?" My arm draped her shoulders, and her head rested on my chest.

"No."

"Yes, he did. He kept you hostage."

She shook her head. "I wasn't a hostage. I was a friend trying to make up for what I'd done to him. Now he's going to have to get along on his own."

"He can do it," I said. "I think his father is really going to be there for him this time. Darin will be better off at college, far away from home, without his mother manipulating his life."

"I don't think she's going to manipulate him anymore," Joy said.

"He didn't really want to die tonight. If he did, he would've waited till we were gone before dumping himself into the pool. Sometimes I hate him, but I feel so sorry for him."

"He'll probably get psychotherapy. That might help him a lot."

"Maybe that's what he needed all along."

"We should try to see him tomorrow," Joy said.

"All right."

She shivered again, and I kissed her forehead till she stopped. "What was the arrangement, the deal you had with Mrs. Steele?"

She blew out a long breath. "Mrs. Steele hated me for a long while after Darin's accident. I didn't blame her. Whenever I came to visit at the hospital—she was there all the time—and she got me alone, she called me everything she could think of: bitch, whore, slut. She said what happened was my fault. I begged her not to tell my parents. I'd do anything. A few days after it happened, when we all knew how serious the accident had been, she told me Darin was going to be helpless. He would always need someone."

"She laid a guilt trip on you, is what she did."

"I felt so ashamed, so guilty, I would have agreed to anything. She said she could sue my parents."

"That's crazy. On what grounds?"

"I don't know."

"She intimidated you."

"She might have tried to sue. I didn't know. I was so scared. My parents don't have any money. Everything would've been in the paper. Daddy works at the paper; Mom's a teacher. How could I put them through such a mess? Everyone in town would've known how I ruined Darin Steele's life."

"He got himself drunk, Joy. Don't forget that. He has to accept responsibility."

"I told Mrs. Steele I'd be there for Darin as long as he needed me."

"She blackmailed you."

Joy shrugged out of my arms and looked at me. "You still don't get it, do you? I felt staying with him was the right thing to do in the first place. Don't you see? I would have stayed with him even if Mrs. Steele hadn't scared me."

"You're not the only person Mrs. Steele tried to manipulate for Darin's benefit." I told her as quickly and concisely as I could about the moves Mrs. Steele had put on me. "I think she figured if I became involved with her, I wouldn't have time for you."

Joy tilted her head and frowned. "She wanted you to sleep with her?"

"I think so."

"You weren't interested?"

"Hell, no. I love you. I stayed away from her as much as I could." Then another thought crossed my mind. "Did Mr. Steele know what really happened that night?"

"That's when he was always drinking. He was passed out that night. Probably Mrs. Steele told him later."

"Then I came along," I said, "with my wonderful idea—summer sex—and ruined everything."

"I could've said no."

"It was a bad idea."

Joy nodded, her face suddenly sad in the moon-light. "Being pregnant frees me from Darin and his mother but has complicated the future so bad I don't know what's going to happen."

"The fun wasn't worth it," I said. "We hurt our-selves and everyone else."

We sat in silence. An owl hooted from a nearby tree, and we both gave a start, then laughed a little. "Look," I said. "We've got to look at the good side. You pitched a no-hitter and won a state championship game. You'll get tons of scholarship offers."

"What will I do with one?"

"Sit out a year. Then go to college. I'm sure other female athletes turn up pregnant. Colleges probably make concessions."

"A baby, college, softball—how will I manage all three? College classes take lots of work, so does a baby. Ball teams are always traveling. Who will watch the baby? How will I get enough money to meet expenses? It all seems overwhelming. Life was so simple before."

"It's not the end of the world," I said. "We've got to think of the positive things. We've got to sit down with our parents and figure out a way. I'm going to be gone to the navy, but we have a few weeks to plan." I pulled her close again. "It's going to kill me to leave you."

"Your being away four years seems like such a long time."

"I'm never going to let you down, or our baby. I want you to know that."

"Four years . . . What will happen to us in four years? Look at what happened to us in a summer."

"I get thirty days leave every year. It's not like I'll never see you."

"I'm so scared, Jeremy."

"I know. I am, too. But listen: it's important to me that I be a major part of your life and the baby's life. Believe me."

I told her the story of Mom and me, of my never having known my father, so she'd understand why I'd always be there for her and the baby.

My story shocked her. She looked at me sadly and touched my cheek where she'd hit me. "You, Darin, me—life hasn't played very fair, has it?"

"The game's not over," I said. "We haven't lost."

I kissed her, then looked at my watch in the moonlight.

"It's one-thirty," I said. "I'm sure a few parties are roaring by now." Going to a party was the last thing I felt like doing, but this was the biggest night of Joy's softball career. She had a right to a party if she wanted one.

"What do you say? Party time?"

"I don't think so, Jeremy."

"You don't have to drink," I said. "You can soak up cheers, applause, and congratulations. You owe it to yourself."

Joy shook her head. "I'm not interested. I'm sorry. I'm really not."

"Me, neither, to tell the truth. I just thought I'd ask." Taking her in my arms again, I rested my chin on the top of her head. "So much has happened tonight, partying seems pointless."

"A waste of time," she said.

"Let's get your car."

I drove Joy to her car at the Steeles' house, then followed her home. Later, on the porch swing, I kissed her good night. Good morning, really, though it was still dark, stars shining. Later in the day, we would have to tell her parents everything.